John Payne

New Poems

John Payne

New Poems

ISBN/EAN: 9783337398019

Printed in Europe, USA, Canada, Australia, Japan

Cover: Foto ©Andreas Hilbeck / pixelio.de

More available books at **www.hansebooks.com**

BY

JOHN PAYNE.

LONDON :
NEWMAN AND CO.,
43, HART STREET, OXFORD STREET.
1880.

TO

THE BELOVED MEMORY

OF

THÉOPHILE GAUTIER.

CONTENTS.

LIKE as the sunflower lifts up to the sun
     Its star of summer, in the noontide heat,
Following the sacred circuit of his feet,
What while towards the house of Night they run;
Nor when the glad Day's glory is fordone
And the sun ceases from the starry street,
It leaves to turn to his celestial seat,
Seeking his face behind the shadows dun;

Even so my heart, from out these darkling days,
Whose little light is sad for winter's breath,
Strains upward still—with song and prayer and praise
Ensuing ever, through the gathering haze,
Those twin suns of our darkness—Love and Death—
That rule the backward and the forward ways.

TOURNESOL.

A Prelude.

GEOFFREY OF RUDEL ! How the name
    Leaps to the lips like a flower of flame,
  Holding the heart with a dream of days
  When life lay yet in the flowered ways
And the winds of the world were stirred and strong
With blast of battle and silver of song !
  When love was long and women were true
  And the bell of the steadfast sky was blue
Over a world that was white as yet
From load of labour and fruitless fret
  Of hunger for gain and greed of gold,
  That now have made us our young world old !
I hail thee, honest and tender time !
I, last of many, that with rude rhyme
  Ring out reproach to the cheerless air
  And chide the age that it is not fair.

And first of any the blames I bring,
I chide it for lack of love-liking,
　　For fall of faith and hope grown cold,
　　For love turned lusting and youth grown old.
For where, I pray you, in this our day
Dwells there the lover that loves alway ?
　　And where is the lady whose constant eye
　　Shall seek one only until she die ?
Alack ! for Rudel and Carmosine,
Whose love, as the constant sun his sheen,
　　Burns like a beryl in lays of yore !
　　Their day is dead as the bale they bore
For faithful fancy ; and now alone
In minstrels' making their name is known.
　　Their thought is perished, their peerless fame
　　Faded and past as the marish flame
That flees from the blink of the breaking day ;
And love is dead with them—wel-a-way !
　　For now men's love is a fitful fire,
　　A wayless desert of waste desire ;
And women's love is a cold caprice,
A wind that changes withouten cease.
　　For the lifelong love that in days of old
　　Was dearer than lands and grain and gold,

The love that possessed men's heart and soul
In life and liesse, in death and dole—
 That stirred their spirits to many a deed
 Of noble daring,—that was the meed
Of haughty honour and high emprize,—
That made men look in their lady's eyes
 For gain and guerdon of all their strife,—
 This love lack we in our modern life.
For the folk through the fretful hours are hurled
On the ruthless rush of the wondrous world,
 And none has leisure to lie and cull
 The blossoms that made life beautiful,
In that old season when men could sing
For dear delight in the risen Spring
 And Summer ripening fruit and flower.
 Now carefulness cankers every hour;
We are too weary and sad to sing;
Our pastime's poisoned with thought-taking.
 The bloom is faded from all that's fair,
 And grey with smoke is the grievous air.
None lifts to luting his hand and voice
Nor smites the strings with a joyful noise;
 For all that sing in the land are pale;
 Their voice is the voice of those that wail

For beauty buried, and hang the head
For the dream of a day evanishèd.

How shall we say sweet things in rhyme
Of this our marvellous modern time,
We that are heavy at heart to sing,
But may not rejoice for remembering?
We care not, we, for the gorgeous glow
Of wealth and wonder, the stately show
Of light and luxury, that sweeps past,
Unheeded, before our eyes downcast.
The pageant of passion and pride and crime
That fills the face of the turncoat time,
The gold that glitters, the gems that glow,
Hide not from us the wasting woe
That gnaws at the heart of the hungry age.
The starving soul in the crystal cage
Looks through the loop of the blazoned bars,
As out of heaven the sorrowing stars
Gaze on the grief of the night newborn.

What shall we do for the world forlorn,
We that drink deep of its sorrowing?
What can we do, alas! but sing?

Sing as the bird behind the wire,
That pours out his passion of dear desire,
His fret for the forest far away,
His hunger of hope for the distant day
    When peradventure shall ope for him
    The door that darkens on heaven's rim—
What can we do, bird-like, but pour
Into our singing the dreams of yore,
    The long desire of the soul exiled
    From some sweet Eden grown waste and wild?
And if, by fortune, we turn our feet,
Torn with long travel, towards that sweet,
    That happy haven of "long ago,"
    And tune our lutany soft and low
To some dear ditty of things that were,
Memoried with melodies faint and fair,
    Shall any blame us for this that we
Fordid time's tyranny, and forgot
Awhile life's lovelessness?   I trow not;
    For song is sinless, and fancy free.

A FUNERAL SONG FOR THÉOPHILE GAUTIER.*

W HAT shall our song be for the mighty dead,
    For this our master that is ours no more ?
  Lo ! for the dead was none of those that wore
The laurel lightly on a heedless head,
Chanting a song of idle lustihead
    Among the sun-kissed roses on the shore !
    This our belovèd, that is gone before,
Was of the race of heroes battle-bred
That, from the dawn-white to the sunset-red,
            Fought in the front of war !

Lo ! this was he that in the weary time,
    In many a devious and darkling way,
    Through dusk of doubt and thunder of dismay,
Held our hearts hopeful with his resonant rhyme,
Lifting our lives above the smoke and slime

     ' Written for " Le Tombeau de Théophile Gautier."

Into some splendid summer far away,
Where the sun brimmed the chalice of the day
With gold of heaven, and the accordant chime
Of woods and waters to the calm sublime
      Carolled in roundelay !

This was our poet in the front of faith ;
  Our singer gone to his most sweet repose,
  Sped to his summer from our time of snows
And winter winding all the world with death.
Who shall make moan or utter mournful breath
  That this our noblest one no longer knows
  Our evil place of toil and many woes,
Lying at the last where no voice entereth ?
Who shall weave for him other than a wreath
      Of laurel and of rose ?

Hence with the cypress and the funeral song !
  Let not the shrill sound of our mourning mar
  His triumph that upon the Immortals' car
Passes, star-crowned ; but from the laurelled throng
That stand await, let every voice prolong

A noise of jubilance that from afar
Shall hail in heaven the new majestic star
That rises with a radiance calm and strong,
To burn for ever unobscured among
        The courts where the Gods are !

Ay, let the trumpets and the clarions blow,
  The air rain roses, and the sky resound
  With harpings of his peers that stand around,
What while the splendours of the triumph go
Along the streets and through the portico !
  I too, who loved the dead, as from the ground
  The glow-worm loves the star, will stand, brow-
    bound
With winter-roses, in the sunset-glow,
And make thin music, fluting soft and low
        Above his funeral mound.

I too, who loved him, from beyond the sea
  Add my weak note to that sublime acclaim
  That, soaring with the silver of his name,
Shall shake the heavens with splendid harmony,
Till all who listen bend in awe the knee,

Seeing a giant's spirit, like a flame,
Remounting to that heaven from which it came,
And many weep for very shame to see
The majesty they knew not till 'twas free
From earthly praise or blame.

Hail, O our master !   From the hastening hours
This one we set above its grey-veiled peers,
Armed with thy name against the night that nears !
We crown it with the glory of the flowers,
We wind it with all magic that is ours
Of song and hope and jewel-coloured tears ;
We charm it with our love from taint of fears ;
We set it high against the sky that lowers,
To burn, a love-sign, from the topmost towers,
Through glad and sorry years.

CHANT ROYAL OF THE GOD
OF LOVE.

O MOST fair God ! O Love both new and old,
    That wert before the flowers of morning blew,
Before the glad sun in his mail of gold
    Leapt into light across the first day's dew,
That art the first and last of our delight,
That in the blue day and the purple night
    Holdest the hearts of servant and of king,
    Lord of liesse, sovran of sorrowing,
That in thy hand hast heaven's golden key,
    And hell beneath the shadow of thy wing,
Thou art my Lord to whom I bend the knee !

What thing rejects thy mastery ? Who so bold
    But at thine altars in the dusk they sue ?
Even the strait pale Goddess, silver-stoled,
    That kissed Endymion when the spring was new,
To thee did homage in her own despite,
When in the shadow of her wings of white

She slid down trembling from her moonèd ring
To where the Latmian youth lay slumbering,
And in that kiss put off cold chastity.
Who but acclaim, with voice and pipe and string,
Thou art my Lord to whom I bend the knee?

Master of men and gods, in every fold
Of thy wide vans, the sorceries that renew
The labouring earth tranced with the winter's cold
Lie hid, the quintessential charms that woo
The souls of flowers, slain with the sullen might
Of the dead year, and draw them to the light.
Balsam and blessing to thy garments cling:
Skyward and seaward, whilst thy white palms fling
Their spells of healing over land and sea,
One shout of homage makes the welkin ring,
Thou art my Lord to whom I bend the knee!

I see thee throned aloft: thy fair hands hold
Myrtles for joy, and euphrasy and rue:
Laurels and roses round thy white brows rolled,
And in thine eyes the royal heaven's hue:
But in thy lips' clear colour, ruddy bright,
The heart's blood shines of many a hapless wight.

Thou art not only fair and sweet as Spring :
Terror and beauty, fear and wondering,
Meet on thy front, amazing all who see. —
All men do praise thee—ay, and every thing !
Thou art my Lord to whom I bend the knee !

I fear thee, though I love.   Who can behold
The sheer sun burning in the orbèd blue,
What while the noontide over hill and wold
Flames like a fire, except his mazèd view
Wither and tremble ?   So thy splendid sight
Fills me with mingled gladness and affright.
Thy visage haunts me in the wavering
Of dreams, and in the dawn, awakening,
I feel thy splendour streaming full on me.
Both joy and fear unto thy feet I bring :
Thou art my Lord to whom I bend the knee !

ENVOI.

God above gods, High and Eternal King !
Whose praise the symphonies of heaven sing,
I find no whither from thy power to flee
Save in thy pinions' vast o'ershadowing :
Thou art my Lord to whom I bend the knee !

WITH A COPY OF HENRY VAUGHAN'S SACRED POEMS.

L AY down thy burden at this gate and knock.
 What if the world without be dark and drear ?
 For there be fountains of refreshment here
Sweeter than all the runnels of the rock.
Hark ! even to thy hand upon the lock
 A wilding warble answers, loud and clear,
 That falls as fain upon the heart of fear
As shepherds' songs unto the folded flock.

This is the quiet wood-church of the soul.
Be thankful, heart, to him betimes that stole,
 Some Easter morning, through the golden door—
Haply ajar for early prayer to rise—
 And brought thee back from that song-flowered
 shore
These haunting harmonies of Paradise.

THE BALLAD OF THE KING'S ORCHARD.

*From Theodore de Banville.**

H ERE, where wakens the flowering year,
 The forest bears on its boughs a score
Of dead folk hanged by the neck ; and sheer
 Gold of the dawn on them doth pour.
 Strangest fruits ever forest bore
Under the oak-boughs hang in a string,
 Fruits unheard of by Turk or Moor :
It is the orchard of Louis the King.

* This ballad, together with its companion "The Ballad
of the Common Folk" (see "Songs of Life and Death,"
1872), was, at the express request of M. de Banville, translated
in 1871 for M. Aublet's English adaptation of "Gringoire,"
which it was then in contemplation to produce at a London
Theatre.

All the poor devils shrivelling here,
　Thinking thoughts silent for evermore,
Dance in a hurly-burly drear,
　With hearts whose panting is hardly o'er :
　The sun-heat burns and scorches them sore :
Wondering heavens, see how they swing
　In the dawn-glow growing behind and before !
It is the orchard of Louis the King.

Hanged poor folk, in the devil's ear,
　They call for more gallows-fruit and more—
Call and call, whilst the sky grows clear
　And the dews float up from the forest floor,
　Through the air that glitters like Heaven's door :
Round their heads flapping and fluttering,
　Chatter and peck at them birds galore :
It is the orchard of Louis the King.

ENVOI.

Prince, I know of a wood where store
　Of hanged poor folk to the branches cling,
Lapt and shrouded in leafage hoar :
　It is the orchard of Louis the King.

J. B. COROT.

Died 22nd February, 1875.

BEFORE the earliest violet he died,—
   That loved the new green and the stress of Spring
   So tenderly !   He knew that March must bring
The primrose by the brook, and all the wide
Green spaces of the forest glorified
   With scent and singing, when each passing wing
   Would call him and each burst of blossoming:
He knew he could not die in the Spring-tide.

Yet he was weary, for his task was done,
   And sleep seemed sweet unto the tired eyes:
Weary ! for many a year he had seen the sun
      Arise; so in the season of the snows
      He put off life—ere Spring could interpose
   To hold him back—and went where Gautier lies.

THORGERDA.

THORGERDA.

Voices in the Air.

THE night is riven from earth and heaven ;
   The day is blue in the sweet sky-dome ;
The glad sea glimmers with soft sun-shimmers ;
   The white sea fairies float on the foam.

The storm has faded from day new-braided
   With webs of azure above the seas :
Shore-spirits, come, whilst the blast is dumb,
   And the seaflowers sway to the fragrant breeze.

I hear a ringing of sea-nymphs' singing,
   Far out to sea in the golden haze :
Sweet sisters, haste, ere the noon have chased
   The cool-haired dawn from the sweet sea-ways.

The air is golden ; the storm is holden
   In sapphire chains of the sleepless stars :
I see the flashing of mermaidens plashing
   And merrows glinting in sea-shell cars.

Come swift, sweet sisters !   Our witch-wife trysters
   Will soon in the distance fade and flee :
Wide-winged we travel through the thin foam-ravel,
   To ride on the weed-weft mane of the sea.

The Witch.

1.

L O ! what a golden day it is !
    The glad sun rives the sapphire deeps
Down to the dim pearl-floored abyss
    Where, cold in death, my lover sleeps ;

Crowns with soft fire his sea-drenched hair,
    Kisses with gold his lips death-pale,
Lets down from heaven a golden stair,
    Whose steps methinks his soul doth scale.

This is my treasure.   White and sweet,
    He lies beneath my ardent eyne,
With heart that never more shall beat,
    Nor lips press softly against mine.

How like a dream it seems to me,
    The time when hand-in-hand we went
By hill and valley, I and he,
    Lost in a trance of ravishment !

I and my lover here that lies
   And sleeps the everlasting sleep,
We walked whilere in Paradise ;
   (Can it be true ?)   Our souls drank deep

Together of Love's wonder-wine :
   We saw the golden days go by,
Unheeding, for we were divine ;
   Love had advanced us to the sky.

And of that time no traces bin,
   Save the still shape that once did hold
My lover's soul, that shone therein,
   As wine laughs in a vase of gold,

Cold, cold he lies, and answers not
   Unto my speech ; his mouth is cold
Whose kiss to mine was sweet and hot
   As sunshine to a marigold.

And yet his pallid lips I press ;
   I fold his neck in my embrace ;
I rain down kisses none the less
   Upon his unresponsive face :

I call on him with all the fair
    Flower-names that blossom out of love ;
I knit sea-jewels in his hair ;
    I weave fair coronals above

The cold sweet silver of his brow ;
    For this is all of him I have ;
Nor any Future more than now
    Shall give me back what Love once gave.

For from Death's gate our lives divide ;
    His was the Galilean's faith :
With those that serve the Crucified,
    He shared the chance of Life and Death.

And so my eyes shall never light
    Upon his star-soft eyes again ;
Nor ever in the day or night,
    By hill or valley, wood or plain,

Our hands shall meet afresh.   His voice
    Shall never with its silver tone
The sadness of my soul rejoice,
    Nor his breast throb against my own.

His sight shall never unto me
  Return whilst heaven and earth remain :
Though Time blend with Eternity,
  Our lives shall never meet again.

Never by grey or purple sea,
  Never again in heavens of blue,
Never in this old earth—ah me
  Never, ah never ! in the new.

For he, he treads the windless ways
  Among the thick star-diamonds,
Where in the middle æther blaze
  The golden City's pearl gate-fronds ;

Sitteth, palm-crowned and silver-shod,
  Where in strange dwellings of the skies
The Christians to their Woman-God
  Cease nevermore from psalmodies.

And I, I wait, with haggard eyes
  And face grown awful for desire,
The coming of that fierce day's rise
  When from the cities of the fire

The wolf shall come with blazing crest,
  And many a giant armed for war ;
When from the sanguine-streaming West,
  Hell-flaming, speedeth Naglfar.*

II.

I was a daughter of the race
  Of those old gods the Christians hurled
From their high heaven-hilled dwelling-place,
  Gladsheimr, poised above the world.

My mother was the fairest child
  The Norse-land knew—so strangely fair,
The very gods looked down and smiled
  At her clear eyes and lucent hair.

And Thor the Thunderer, enspelled
  By hunger of a god's desire
For mortal love, came down, compelled
  And did possess her like a fire.

---

* The enchanted ship, in which, according to the Norse mythology, the Jötuns, or giants, and the demons that dwell in Muspelheim (the land of fire) shall at the last day sail over sea and land, led by the Fenris-wolf and the Midgard serpent, to the assault of Asgard, the dwelling of the gods.

And from the love of god and maid
　　There was a child of wonder born,
On whom the gods for guerdon laid
　　Gifts goodlier than lands and corn.

There was to her the queendom given
　　O'er all the sprites of earth and sea,
O'er every wind that rends the heaven,
　　All lightnings through the clouds that flee.

Gifts did they give to her for flight
　　Athwart the crystal waves of air,
To cleave the billows green and white
　　And float among the sea-nymphs fair.

Her eyes pierced all the veils of mist
　　And all the crannies of the sea :
There was no hill-cave but she wist
　　To master all its mystery.

And since she was the last of all
　　The godlike race upon the earth
That could endure the Christian's thrall,
　　Being so mingled in her birth,

A spell was laid upon her life,
　　A charm of thunder and of fire,
That she should wage an endless strife,
　　For Thor the Thunderer's sake, her sire,

With that pale god, the Nazarene,
　　And all his servants on the earth,
Smite all their days with dole and teen
　　And waste their every work with dearth ;

For that alone by sea and land
　　She should do battle for the gods
And for the Æsir* champion stand,
　　Far banished from the green Norse sods.

That child was I, Thorgerda hight'
　　For memory of my mighty sire,
The last one of those maids of might
　　That ruled the fiends of air and fire.

III.

I am the old gods' sword-bearer :
　　Upon this world of life and death,
Alone against the Christ I rear
　　The standard of the ancient faith :

---

* *Æsir*, the Northern gods, so called from their supposed
Asian origin.

I am their champion, that do wage
  Unending and remorseless war
Against the new and barren age
  That knows not Odin—no, nor Thor.

I am the witch of Norroway,
  The sorceress that rides the blast,
That sends the whirlwind on its way
  To rend the sail and snap the mast.

By day and night, by sea and land,
  I wreak on men unnumbered ills ;
I hurl the thunder from my hand,
  I pour the torrent from the hills.

I stand upon the height of heaven
  And smite the world with pestilence ;
The Christ and his Archangels seven
  Cannot prevail against me thence.

But more especially the night
  Is given to me to work my will :
Therein, with ravening delight,
  Of ruin red I take my fill.

When as the sun across the wave
   Has drawn the colour from the sky,
And over all the dead day's grave
   The grisly night mounts wide and high,.

My heart throbs loud, my wings expand,
   I rush, I soar into the air,
And, falcon-like, o'er sea and land,
   Valley and hill, I fly and fare.

I hover o'er the haunts of men,
   Above the white town-dotted coasts,
The hollow, moon-bemaddened glen,
   Brimmed with the bodiless grey ghosts.

I scatter curses far and near,
   I fill the air with deaths that fly :
The pale folk tremble as they hear
   My rushing wings that hurtle by.

And often when the world is white
   Beneath the moon, and all things sleep,
I wake the storm-fiends in the night
   And loose the whirlwind o'er the deep.

I sink the great ships on the sea,
   I grip the seamen by the hair
And drag them strangling down with me
   To drown among the corals rare.

I bid the volleying thunders roar,
   The lightnings leap, the rushing rain
Swell up the sea against the shore,
   To overwhelm the fated plain.

I stand upon the hills and hurl
   The crashing thunderbolts afar,
Until the wild waves in their swirl
   Blot out the sight of moon and star.

I slay the cattle in the stall,
   I smite the sheep upon the fells;
The great pines in the forest fall,
   Stricken and blasted by my spells.

The Christians call upon their God,
   That cannot ward them from my power:
No living thing dares stir abroad
   When as I rule the midnight hour.

No man that meets me in the night,
   But he is numbered with the dead :
The world until the morning light
   Is given to me for death and dread.

But when the break of morning-grey
   The cloudwrack in the east divides
And wan and woeful comes the day,
   The tempest in my soul subsides ;

And weary with the night's turmoil,
   I seek some middle mountain cave,
Where sleep falls down on me like oil
   Poured out upon the whirling wave.

Or else I cleave the glancing glass
   Of the still sea, and through the deep
Down to some sea-nymph's grotto pass,
   Whereas the quiet corals sleep,

Unheeding if the sky is blue
   Or if the storm in heaven is seen :
No whisper of the wind sinks through
   The ceiling of that deep serene.

Sometimes, when heaven, frowning-browed,
   Hangs o'er the earth a leaden dome,
I cleave the canopy of cloud
   And in the middle æther roam ;

Seeking some token of my race,
   Some sign to fill my void desire,
So haply I may see the face
   Of Odin or my dreadful sire.

But vast and void the æther lies ;
   My wings arouse no echo there,
Nor my songs, ringing through the skies,
   Evoke an answer from the air.

Blank is the world : there seems no sign
   Of all that was ; the days forget
The gods that drank the wonder-wine
   Of Freya's* grapes whilere.   And yet

Behind the setting, now and then,
   I see a crown of flame and smoke
Burn up above the fiery fen
   Wherein, until the sable cloak

---

* *Freya*, the Northern Venus, who prepared from grapes or apples the drink that gave the gods eternal youth.

Of Time from sea and land be torn
   And the God's Twilight* fill the sky,
The Jötuns 'gainst the battle-morn
   Forge weapons everlastingly.

And in my journeyings through the night
   Across the billows' rushing race,
Midmost the main, far out of sight
   Of land, I come upon a place

Where in mid-ocean, storm-possest,
   When with the sky the stern sea wars,
The Snake† lifts up his horrid crest
   And hisses to the pallid stars.

Bytimes, too, as cold-eyed I sail
   Across the wastes of middle air,
A blithe breeze wafts aside the veil
   Of clouds heaped up and floating there ;

And dimly through the rift of blue
   Turrets and hill-peaks I discern,
And for a space behold anew
   The golden gates of Asgard burn.

* *Ragnärok*, the end of the world.
† The Midgard-serpent, that lies coiled around the world.

And as the vision grows, meseems
  Valhalla rises, grey and wide;
And dim and vast as thunder-dreams,
  The old gods gather side by side.

Upon his throne of elfin gold
  Allfather Odin sits : his beard
Streams o'er his bosom, fold on fold,
  Like mosses on an oak bolt-seared.

And all the gods around him stand,
  Forset, Frey, Balder—ay, the dead
Joined to the live, an awful band :
  And in the midst, with drooping head,

The semblance of my mighty sire,
  Leant on his hammer, stands apart,
His sunk eyes gleaming like the fire
  That glows within some mountain's heart.

A golden glimmer cleaves the gloom;
  And momently, as if there rose
The sun upon some giant's tomb,
  The haloed hair of Freya glows.

3

On Odin's breast she lies and sleeps,
    Whilst to his left, and to his right,
A Valkyr armed the wild watch keeps,
    By Friga, sitting stern and white.

Anon a Raven* stirs and shakes
    His sable wings athwart the hall ;
And for a second Freya wakes,
    And in their sleep the gods stir all :

And Thor lifts up his sunken head
    And poises in his shadowy hand
His awful hammer ; but, outspread,
    Sleep falls again upon the band.

The Raven folds his wings anew ;
    The gleam of Freya's hair fades out ;
And suddenly as first they drew,
    The clinging cloud-wreaths fold about

The City of the sevenfold Hill.
    But I am glad for many a year :
For I have seen the gods live still,
    And looked on Thor the Thunderer.

---

* Odin was fabled to have two Ravens, Thought and Memory, who brought him tidings of all that went on in the world.

And yet but seldom do the gods
  Bow down unto my long desire :
But seldom in the sunset nods
  Odin or Asa-Thor* my sire

Strides on before me through the din
  Of thunders in the midnight wild ;
Nor on the hills the Nornas† spin :
  The gods are angry with their child.

Thor hides his visage from his maid
  For that, some little space whilere
Of days and nights, aside she laid
  Her mission terrible and fair

And stooped to love as women love,
  But fiercelier far than woman can,
The eagle pairing with the dove,
  The heaven-born mating with a man.

IV.

It chanced, one summer's night of blue,
  When nought but stars in heaven were,
And, like a rain of pearls, the dew
  Slid through the golden August air,

* The Asian Thor, the special title of the Thunder-god.
† Nornas, the Northern Fates.

My wings had borne me from the sea
   To where the curving down sloped slow
Into a cirque of lilied lea,
   Whereon sheep wandered to and fro.

Laid in the lap of cliff and hill,
   The velvet down seemed fast asleep
Save for the murmur of a rill
   That trickled past the browsing sheep.

And now and then the herd-bells broke
   The sleep of sound; and faint and far,
The ripple of the sea-surge woke
   A drowsy echo.   Not a star

Twinkled; but in the drowsy dream
   Of hill and down, it was as if
No storm was aye; and it did seem
   No breakers roared behind the cliff.

The charm of peace that brooded there
   Weighed on my wings; and wearywise
I floated on the quiet air,
   Under the dreamy evening skies.

For momently the fierce delight
   Of storm and vengeance died in me ;
And some desire rose in my spright
   Of rest and peace in days to be.

I was aweary of long strife :
   The passion of my awful sire,
That had informed my lonely life
   To wreak on men his dread desire,

Seemed weakening in me ; and instead,
   The earthly part in me arose,
Like to some fire that shows its head
   Of flame above the boreal snows :

And as the keen heat melts the ice
   And drives the winter-woe away,
So in my heart's fierce fortalice
   Awhile the woman's wish held sway.

The godlike part in me awhile
   Fainted; and in my woman's breast
The memory of my mother's smile
   The empty place of hate possessed.

And many a longing, vague and sweet,
  Welled up like fountains in the spring :
My heart glowed with a human heat,
  And in my thought new hopes took wing.

Wish woke in me to put away
  The wonted stress of doom and power,
That gave me empire o'er the day
  And night in every changing hour

And made my soul a scathing fire,
  An immortality of death ;
And therewithal the soft desire
  To breathe the kindly human breath,

To know the charm in life that lies,
  To be no longer curst and lone,
To meet the glance of kindred eyes
  And feel warm lips upon my own.

And as I wavered, half aswoon
  With anguish of unformed desire,
The silver presence of the moon
  Rose in the silence.   High and higher

Into the quiet sky she soared ;
   And as she lit the tranquil sheep
And the pale plain, upon the sward
   I saw the shepherd lie asleep.

Upon a little knoll he lay,
   With face upturned towards the sky,
Bareheaded ; and the breeze at play
   Stirred in his hair caressingly.

The sudden sight to me did seem
   The clear fulfilment of my thought,
As if at ending of a dream
   The half-seen hope to shape were wrought

And day informed the wish of night :
   For he was young and passing fair,
A very angel of delight,
   With sleep-sealed eyes and floating hair.

And as I gazed upon him, lo !
   The fierceness of the first love smote
The age-old ice in me with throe
   On throe of passion : I forgot

My destiny in that sweet hour,
  And all my birth had doomed me to,
Allfather Odin and his power.
  The stars stood in that night of blue

And spoke of nought but love fulfilled,
  And sweets of life with life new knit:
And through their glamour grave and stilled,
  Love spoke and bade me worship it.

I could but yield: the hot blood welled
  Like balms of fire through heart and brain:
My every motion seemed compelled
  To some strange ecstasy of pain,

So sharp and sweet the new wish was:
  And as it grew, my tired wings closed,
And down I sank upon the grass,
  Hard by the place where he reposed.

Then, drunken with a fearful bliss,
  I clasped my arms about his breast,
And in the passion of a kiss,
  My lips upon his lips I press'd.

The hot touch burnt me like a flame :
And he with a great start awoke
And (for sleep still his sense did claim
And the dream held him) would have broke

The prison of my clasping arms :
But could not, for aloud I cried
The softest, sweetest of my charms ;
And as I chanted, white and wide,

My glad wings opened, and I rose
Into the middle midnight air,
Like some night-hawk that homeward goes,
Bearing a culver to its lair.

The breeze sang past me, as I clave
The crystals of the sky serene ;
And presently the plashing wave
Sounded, and past the marge of green

The long blue lapses of the main
Swept to the dawnward, and the foam
Slid up and fled and rose again,
Like white birds wheeling in the gloam.

Down through the deeps of yielding blue
   I plunged with that fair youth I bore,
Harmless, until we sank unto
   Where through the dusk the golden floor

And pearl-hung ceiling of a cave
   Opened upon the sombre sea :
But by my charms the whirling wave
   Drew back and left the entry free.

Therein upon a bank of sand,
   Bordered with corals white and red,
I laid my lover.   Cold his hand
   Was, and his face cold as the dead,

And the lids fallen upon his eyes :
   But soon my sorceries had drawn
The life back; and like some sweet skies
   That break blue underneath the dawn,

His clear eyes opened on my own ;
   The life-blood gathered in his cheek,
And gradually his sweet face shone,
   And his lips moved as if to speak :

For at the first he saw me not;
   But his eyes moved from side to side
Of that pearl-floored and golden grot,
   As if with wonder stupefied.

Then, as they rested on my place,
   At first, the pallor of affright
Drew all the rose-blush from his face
   And made its brilliance marble-white.

But soon, assured that I was fair,
   (For of a truth new-born desire
Had bathed my beauty in a rare
   Splendour as of ethereal fire)

A slow smile gathering on his lips
   Broke into brightness, as the sun,
After some quickly-past eclipse,
   Grows golden through the darkness dun.

His blue eyes glittered with soft light,
   And on his forehead's lambent snow,
The angel of a new delight
   Brooded with pinions all aglow.

The passion in my veins that burned
    Passed to his own like magic wine :
He raised himself with mouth that yearned
    And eyes that fastened upon mine.

Then, as insensibly I drew
    Nearer to him, moved by the spell,
About my neck his arms he threw,
    And on each other's breast we fell.

The dawn aroused me.   To the dome
    Of purple sea that ceiled our cave,
The lances of the light struck home
    Across the emerald-hearted wave.

Through weed and pearl the sheer sun smote
    And turned the gloom of middle sea
To liquid amber, mote on mote,
    Threading the air with jewelry.

And as the many-coloured rays
 Played on his face, I leant my head
Upon my hand and fed my gaze
 Upon my lover's goodlihead.

Long, long I gazed on him, entranced
 With wonderment of dear delight,
Until the frolic motes, that glanced
 Across his eyelids, waxed so bright

That needs his sleep must yield to it.
 His fair face quivered, and his hand
Drew out of mine that folded it.
 And then, as if some soft wind fanned

The petals of a flower apart,
 That in their snowy bell confine
The dewy azure of its heart,
 His blue eyes opened full on mine.

Once more the look of wonderment
 Rose in their depths; but ere it grew
Fulfilled, its faint beginning blent
 Into a sun-sweet smile that knew

No thought save of perfected love
　　And happiness too sweet for speech ;
And in that greeting our hands clove
　　And our lips grew each unto each.

Voices in the Air.

We are glad for the golden birth of the noon,
　　We are filled with the fragrant breath of the breeze
　　The Day-god walks on the woof of the seas ;
The green deeps laugh to his shining shoon ;
And far in the fair sea-shadow the tune
　　Of harps and singings flutters and flees :
The sea-nymphs call us to follow soon,
　　To revel with them in the liquid leas.

All hail, sweet singers !　We follow fast !
　　We follow to float on the white wave-run.
　　We stay but to finish the spells begun,
To rivet the chains of the bounden blast,
To seal the storm in the sea-caves vast
　　With the last few charms that are yet undone :
Then hey ! for the plains where the whale sails past
　　And the white sea-nixes sport in the sun !

All hail ! the sweet of the day is ours !

   Our wings are wet with the salt of the sea !

   Our task is over, our feet are free

To fare where the foam-bells shiver in showers

And the seaweeds glitter with glory of flowers.

   The lines of the land do faint and flee :

We come to the heart of the mid-sea bowers

   On the race of the running billows' glee !

What power shall let us ?   Our lives are light ;

   Our hearts beat high with the laugh of the day !

   We have sundered our souls from the dawning grey ;

We have done with the dream of the darksome night ;

We have set our face to the foam-line white,

   To dream in the nooning the hours away,

Where the sea-swell heaves, and the spray is bright,

   And the petrels wheel in the mid sea-way !

The Witch.

V.

My life put on from that sweet hour
　　Another nature : thence, no more
I thought to wield my baleful power,
　　Nor treasures of my dreadful lore.

There was no magic now for me
　　In stirring up the stormy strife
'Twixt heaven and earth and air and sea :
　　The memory lapsed out of my life

Of my dread mission : faded out
　　Was all my passion of wild hate,
My wrath ancestral, like a rout
　　Of dreams, the sunbeams dissipate.

And I forgot the fearsome spell
　　That scaled my god-born life erewhen
With all the powers of hate and hell
　　To wreak the Æsir's curse on men.

The vengeance of the gods unseen,
　　Whilom with such a fiery smart
Kindled against the Nazarene,
　　No longer rankled in my heart.

The old gods died out of my thought,
　　As though in me they had no share :
The change Love had within me wrought
　　Blotted the past-time from my air.

No more I roamed the affrighted night,
　　Smiting the haunts of men with death,
The hamlets stood, unharmed and white,
　　Unblasted of my burning breath.

No curses slew the wandering folk
　　Belated on the wild sea-moors :
No pines beneath the thunderstroke
　　Crashed down among the trembling boors.

The sea slept calm beneath the sun :
　　No spells of mine across the sky
Unloosed the storm-clouds red and dun,
　　Or hurled the thunders far and nigh.

But full and still the sunlight lay
  Across the lapse of sea and land :
Save for the dancing ripple's play,
  No sea-surge thundered on the sand.

Love had transformed me : now I knew
  None but his strife, no other bliss
Than in my lover's eyes of blue
  To watch the coming of a kiss.

For him, I was an ocean-nymph,
  One of the sweet fantastic kind,
That sport beneath the emerald lymph
  And in their hair sea-corals wind.

Nought could his boyish wisdom read
  Of my weird past within my eyes :
For aye with happy love indeed
  They bathed in dreams of Paradise.

And over all my haughty face
  The glamour of the time had shed
A tender glow of timid grace.
  The splendour of revengeful dread,

That once had marked me, was subdued
  Into a glory faint and fair
That rayed out from my softer mood
  Like sunshine in the April air.

VI.

All day within our cave we slept;
  And when the sunset's scarlet shoon
Over the happy heaven swept,
  And in the faint-hued sky the moon

Mounted,—across the quiet land,
  By hill and valley, wood and dale,
We wandered often, hand-in-hand,
  Under the silver splendour pale.

And often, seated side by side,
  Lost in each other's deep of eyes,
Insensibly the night would glide
  Till morning glittered in the skies.

For nothing but our love we knew
  In earth and air, in sky and sea;
No heaven to my gaze was blue
  As that within his eyes for me.

I could not tire of his fair sight :
  Whenever on his face I fed
My eyes, the first supreme delight
  Relived in all its goodlihead.

And ever, when from sleep I woke
  And saw him lying by my side,
The same sweet wonder on me broke
  As when his beauty first I spied.

Ah me, how fair he was ! Meseems,
  Since God made heaven and earth and air,
He hath not in His wildest dreams
  Made any creature half so fair.

About his forehead's lambent pearl,
  Blushed with the rose-tints of a shell,
The gold locks clustered, curl on curl,
  Like daffodils about the bell

Of some fair haughty lily-cup,
  That in the marges of a wood
Lifts its broad snowy bosom up
  And tempts the bees to light and brood.

And in its eyebrow's arching lines
   Each deep-blue eye seemed, as it were,
A tarn dropped in a curve of pines,
   Upon some snow-white mountain-stair.

What fruit was ever yet so sweet
   As his sweet mouth, where day and night
For me failed never from his seat
   The angel of fulfilled delight.

No sunlight glittered like the smile
   That blossomed from his flower-cup lips ;
Whereat my thirsty soul the while
   Did hover, as a bee that sips.

No snows of silver could compare
   With the white splendour of his breast :
Whilst that my head lay pillowed there,·
   No angel knew a sweeter rest.

His face to me was as a sun
   That smote the winter-thoughts apart,
Scattering old memories every one,
   And made new Springtime in my heart.

Love had brought back the age of gold:
 For me, a new and fairer birth
Had made me radiant, as of old
 Ask* in the Paradisal earth.

It was as if a veil were drawn
 That long had lain before my eyes:
Each hour upon my sense did dawn
 Some splendour new in earth and skies.

The pageants of the sundown burst,
 A new delight, upon my sense:
And night was radiant as the first
 That fell on Embla's* innocence.

The primrose-blooms of daybreak came,
 A new enchantment to my soul:
And noontide, with its flowers of flame,
 Like philters on my passion stole.

Till that sweet time, the silver Spring
 Had come and waned without my heed:
Nor with its flush of blossoming,
 A glory fallen on hill and mead,

---

* Ask and Embla, the Northern Adam and Eve.

The royal Summer had prevailed
  To stir the frost-time in my breast :
Nor yet the Autumn crimson-mailed :
  Winter alone my heart possess'd.

But now each change of land and sea,
  Each cloud that glittered in the sky,
Each flower that opened on the lea,
  Each calling bird that flitted by,

Woke in my breast a new concent
  Of deep delicious harmony :
My soul was grown a lute that blent
  Its note with all sweet sounds that be.

My heart was grown a singing fire
  That with each hour a new sweet strain
Mixed with the many-mingling choir
  Of birds and flowers, of sea and plain.

VII.

My memory fails to count the lapse
  Of time that held our happiness :
So full a mist of glory wraps
  Its golden hours, and such a stress

Of splendour folds it, that meseems
   It might have been as time appears,
That in the dim delight of dreams
   Holds in an hour a thousand years.

For all things yield to love fulfilled :
   To those that walk in Paradise,
The falling feet of Time are stilled ;
   They know not if he creeps or flies.

A moment to their spreading bliss
   May pass a century away ;
Or in the passion of a kiss
   A thousand years be as a day.

Ah me ! though I remembered not
   The seal my birth on me had set,
The wrath of Him that me begot
   And the old gods did not forget.

For evermore some omen sent
   A thrill of anguish through my soul :
Some levin through the clear sky rent ;
   Thor on the mountain-tops did roll.

And now and then, on our delight,
  Across the amber wave would fall
The shadow of a raven's flight :
  The great gods on their child did call

In wailing voices of the storm ;
  And in the sunset's gold and red,
Methought I saw the Thunderer's form
  Grow in the gloaming, dim and dread.

But no sign rankled in my mind :
  Love so possessed my heart and brain,
All else was but an idle wind,
  A passing breath of summer rain.

VIII.

One night, when not a zephyr's breath
  Broke on the deep delicious swoon
Of hill and plain, and still as death,
  The white world slept beneath the moon,

We tracked the quiet stream, that made
  Its silver furrow through the strand
And fell into the sea that played,
  Lapping, upon the curving sand,

Up through wild wood and fern-grown fell
    To where,—a silver thread across
The weeded pebbles,—like a bell,
    Its fountain trickled through the moss.

And parting back the lush sweet growth
    Of waterweeds,—that there did cling,
As if the rivulet were loath
    To yield the secret of its spring,—

Climbing through reed and fern, we found
    Where at the last the young spring shot
Its spire of silver from the ground,
    Midmost a virgin forest-grot.

The clustered clematis hung there,
    Trailed curtain-like the place before,
As if some wood-nymph with her hair
    Had made the grot a fairy door:

And through the tangle wild and sweet
    Of woodbind and convolvulus,
The silver streamlet, in a sheet
    Of crystal multitudinous,

Poured arched above the entering,
　And curving down athwart the roof,
Along the pearly floor did sing,
　Threading between a tangled woof

Of moss and stonecrop, till it slid
　Into a cranny of the stone,
Wherein it seemed the Naïad hid,
　On green of leafage laid alone.

The place was sweet with jasmine-breath :
　Across the silver-spangled grail,
Starred with blue blossoms, wreath on wreath,
　Pervinck and saxifrage did trail.

And in the ultimate recess
　A crowding growth of fragrant thyme
Had made a couch, such as might press
　Some huntress-maid of olden rhyme.

The falling fountain of the stream
　Alone the charmèd silence broke,
Like bell-chimes hearkened in a dream,
　Unknowing if one slept or woke.

The drowsy sweetness of the place
  Stole on our sense ; and we, content,
Gave up ourselves unto that grace
  And mingling charm of sound and scent.

Reclined upon that fragrant bed,
  We lay embraced, perceiving not
Aught but the spell of slumber shed
  From all that sleep-enchanted grot.

And soon the tinkle of the spring
  And the soft cloud of woodland scents,
That in the dreamy air did cling,
  Laid hands of balm upon our sense :

And sleep fell down upon our eyes,
  As softly and unconsciously
As noontide from the August skies
  Falls on the ripple of the sea.

He first did yield him to the charms
  Of that sweet sleep ; and I awhile
Lay gazing on him ; till my arms
  Relaxed, and in my thought his smile

Blent with a dream of summer days;
　And his face seemed to me a flower
That from the marging woodland ways
　Burns in the golden midday hour.

And so sleep fell upon me too;
　The grot died out before my sight:
But yet the stream-song did pursue
　My slumbrous senses, like some light

Chime of sweet bells in Faërie,
　Threading upon a silver string
Of mingling dreams its rosary
　Of pearls.　But as the crystal ring

Murmured unceasing in my ear,
　Dulled with the dream, meseemed it grew
Slowly less sweet, less silver-clear:
　A change across my spirit drew;

And gradually,—as with those
　Upon whose head slow water drops,
Unceasing, till the soft fall grows
　An anguish horrible, that stops

The pulse of life,—so in my brain
  The ceaseless sound of that soft stream
Waxed to a terror and a pain
  Within the chambers of the dream.

Methought at first it was a knell
  That sounded for Love's funeral :
And then, again, its tinkle fell
  Like storm-waves on a cavern wall :

But ever loudlier ; until
  It was the distant-seeming roar
Of thunder, over wood and hill
  Growing and nearing evermore.

Louder and nearer still it came,
  Until meseemed above my head
The bolts broke, and the lightning's flame
  Tore up the heaven with rifts of red.

And in the dream I heard the car
  Of Thor across the hill-tops roll,
Shaking to ruin every star :
  The world trembled from pole to pole

With that fierce clamour, and the air
  Rang with the startled nightbirds' cries.
And as I lay and listened there,
  The Thunderer hurled across the skies

His awful hammer.   Full and straight,
  Meseemed it clove the screaming heaven,
Ruddy as flame, and fierce as fate,
  Full at my lover's brow was driven.

Down at my very feet it fell,
  Flaming, and cleft the quaking ground
Down to the inmost heart of hell :
  And from the rift, a roaring sound

Of fires innumerous burst into
  The midnight air : the very core
Of the abysmal world shone blue
  And awful.   Then again a roar

Of thunders unendurable
  The cloisters of the æther broke,
So terrible that the dream-spell
  Was cloven away, and I awoke.

IX.

The grot was still, save for the sound
  Of waters whispering through the air ;
The moonlight lay along the ground
  And lit my lover sleeping there.

The terror of the dream possess'd
  My waking sense : with fearful ear
I listened, half affrighted lest
  Some horror should be drawing near.

But not a breath the stillness clave :
  The wind was silent : even the sea
Bore not thus far its rippling wave,
  And the birds slept on bush and tree.

Perfected peace held everything.
  And yet there lingered in my head
The terror of remembering :
  A cold sweat over me was shed,

And my heart fainted in my breast :
  I could not conquer with my will
The tremors that upon me press'd,
  The thrill of thunders echoing still.

Some fearful presence seemed to brood
  Above the place. Its every nook
Was lit with moonlight : yet I could
  Awhile not lift my head to look.

At last, moved by some hidden spell,
  I raised my eyes from off the floor;
And where the middle moonlight fell,
  I saw a shadow in the door.

I could nor speak nor move for fear :
  I could but gaze ; and as I gazed,
The shadow darkened and drew near,
  And from its depths two great eyes blazed

Like fiery stars. Darker it grew
  And taller, till the cave was filled
With the weird presence, and I knew
  The awful shape of him that killed

Skadnir ;* for now the dusk had ta'en
  Terror and beauty ; and before
My shrinking sight there stood again
  The figure of the Thunderer Thor,

* A Norse Titan, who scaled Asgard and was slain by Thor.

5

Leant on his hammer.   Not a word
   Came from the god's lips ; but his eyes
Blazed like a bale-fire.   On the ground
   I crouched before him, suppliant-wise,

With hands outstretched in silent dread :
   For in the terror of his look
The anger of the gods I read,
   As in some judgment-angel's book.

But still his eyes of changeless flame
   Burnt on my own ; and as they shot
Their splendours on me, a strange shame
   Rose in me, for that I forgot

The great gods banished from the earth,
   The anguish of my mighty sire
And all the passion of my birth,
   To follow forth a weak desire.

And as I looked upon him, still
   The fulgent glory of his gaze
My every vein and thought did thrill
   With memories of the olden days.

Before their searching light meseemed
  The earthly part fled forth from me ;
And it was but as if I dreamed
  Love and its human ecstasy.

The woman's weakness of desire
  Forsook my brain ; and in its stead,
The old divine revengeful fire
  Rose up within me, fierce and red.

Once more the wild wrath in me burned,
  The passion of ancestral rage :
And once again my spirit yearned
  To loose the storm-winds from their cage,

To cleave the quiet air with doom,
  To ride the thunder through the sky,
To chase the Christians to the tomb
  With lightnings darting far and nigh.

Then as I rose, dreadful and fair
  With that new fearfulness of birth,
The Thunder god waxed brighter there,
  Until it seemed the cowering earth

5—2

Trembled beneath his flaming sight.
 To me he beckoned, and I grew
In stature to my godlike height ;
 And still my steps to him he drew.

And as I strode out of the grot
 And stood beneath the quiet moon,
Behold, I looked and saw him not :
 But in the sky, rune upon rune,

The stars, in characters of blood,
 Shone like a scroll of fate and fear :
And as possessèd there I stood,
 I heard the thunder drawing near.

Then like some fierce volcanic sea,
 The weird possession of my race
Rose, myriad-minded, up in me.
 One after one, like hawks that chase

Each other through the quivering air,
 The spells, that startle from their rest
The tempest-demons in their lair,
 Burst up, tumultuous, from my breast.

And as they winged it south and north,
   The thunder broke across the sky :
The snakes of doom shot hissing forth,
   Crested with bale-fires blue and high.

And from the rifted clouds, that shone
   Livid with sulphur-flames, there fell
Rain, hail and many a blazing stone,
   As though to the sheer heaven hell

Had leapt, and surging o'er the world
   Like to a canopy of doom,
Upon the cowering valleys hurled
   The fires and furies of its womb.

Then my wings spread out wide and white ;
   And through the turmoil I had made,
Drunk with wild wrath, into the night
   I mounted. Many a meteor played,

Crown-like, about my haughty head :
   And as across the sky I swept,
Like serpents following where I led,
   Around my path the lightnings leapt.

From every corner of the sky
  I heard the rush of flaming wings :
The fiends across the world did fly,
  And the air teemed with fearful things.

All demons in the earth that dwell
  Or in the caverns of the sea
Gathered : the grisly ghouls of hell,
  And all the monstrous shapes that be

Within the air and in the fire
  Flocked to my call, to wreak on men
The deadly passion of my sire
  And the old gods : and now and then,

As, on the pinions of the wind,
  Among the dragons I did stride,
With hair that flamed out far behind,
  Methought I saw the Valkyrs ride.

And I the while chanted aloud
  My sternest sorceries and hurled
My deadliest charms abroad and strowed
  A rain of ruin on the world.

Each word I sang, each sign I made,
  Was fraught with terror and affright.
Obedient, the levins rayed,
  The hailstones hurtled through the night.

A flood of fierce destruction rained
  Upon the terror-stricken earth :
The hosts of hell were all unchained
  To whelm the world with death and dearth.

The ocean burst its age-old bounds
  And rushed upon the shuddering shore :
As 'twere a herd of demon-hounds,
  The whirling waves did leap and roar.

And soon no limit marked the place
  Where the sea was and where the plain ;
But over all the prospect's face,
  The raging waters spread amain.

X.

And so all night I rode the blast ;
  And all night long, spell upon spell,
Rang, trumpet-sounded, fierce and fast,
  My summons to the host of hell.

Until across the lurid gloom
    A streak of wavering white was drawn,
And like a grey ghost from the tomb,
    Arose the pale phantasmal dawn.

Then from the world my sorcery ceased ;
    The demons vanished to the dead ;
And at the token in the East,
    The sullen ocean sought its bed.

Into the night the thunders died,
    With wailing echoes o'er the hills ;
And all the snakes of lightning vied
    In flight before the morning's sills.

And then the pallid sun arose,
    Ghastly with horror : like a flame
On funerals its light that throws,
    Across the wasted world it came.

Beneath its rays the earth spread cold
    And stark as in the swoon of death :
The flocks lay dead upon the wold,
    The cattle lifeless on the heath.

The homesteads lay in ruined heaps
    Or stood a void of sea-stained stone,
Save where upon the mountain-steeps
    Some bolt-seared castle rose alone.

And everywhere the folk lay dead,
    Mother by daughter, sire by son :
No live thing seemed to lift its head
    Under the epicedial sun.

Save where, perchance, a shivering group
    Of peasants on some lofty crest,
Whither for safety they did troop,
    Each against each in terror press'd.

No bird-songs hailed the hopeless morn :
    The thrush sat dead upon the tree ;
The lark lay drowned among the corn,
    The cuckoo blasted on the lea.

The forests lay in tangled lines,
    Smitten against the ravaged ground ;
And out to sea, great rooted pines
    Whirled in the eddies round and round.

Upon its seething breast, as 'twere
    The trophies of that night of fear,
The hollow-sounding ocean bare
    The drowned folk floating far and near.

Upon the waves their lank hair streamed
    Like weeds; and in their open eyes,
As on the surge they rocked, meseemed
    I saw the dreams of death arise.

XI.

Above the wrack of death and dread
    I floated—like some bird of prey,
Worn with long rapine— in the dead
    And stillness of the growing day.

And in my heart the fierce delight
    Of ruin and destruction waned;
The drunken madness of the night
    Ebbed; and but weariness remained.

Landward my tired wings carried me,
    Following the rill, that now no more,
A silver ribbon, joined the sea,
    But swollen into a torrent's roar,

Swept raging o'er its rocky bed :
 And as I floated, knowing not
Whither, I saw that chance had led
 My pinions to the river-grot.

All bare it lay : the raging wave
 Had stripped the creepers from the stone,
And in the opening of the cave
 The rocky pillars overthrown.

The silver singing fountain-thread
 Trickled no longer from the door,
An arching crystal : in its stead,
 A foaming flood of water tore

The clinging clematises' woof.
 The place lay open to the sky ;
For in the storm the rocky roof
 Was cloven and scattered far and nigh.

And as I looked upon the waste
 Of what had been so fair a place,
With all its beauty now erased,
 The memory of my lover's face

Smote on my spirit suddenly;
    And in that flash of backward thought,
Remembrance startled up in me
    Of all the change the night had wrought.

The anguish of past love again
    Revived in me; and mad with fear
And love foreboding, I was fain
    To call upon him, loud and clear.

Across the air my shrill cries rang;
    But no voice answered to my own:
Only the calling echoes' clang
    Rose up and died from rock and stone.

Again I called him by his name;
    And still across the quivering air
The hollow-sounding echoes came,
    For sole response to my despair.

Then, dazed with agonized affright,
    I plunged into the surging wave,
That filled up to its utmost height
    The hollow bosom of the cave;

And in the water-darkened grot,
   With trembling hands and pallid face,
Madly I sought but long found not
   My lover in that mournful place.

At last, as in the dusk I groped—
   Probing each innermost recess,
To find I scarce knew what I hoped
   Or feared—a floating tangled tress

Caught in my hands, as 'twere a weed
   That in its flight the water bare :
But as I looked, I saw indeed
   It was my lover's golden hair.

Then diving through the pool of foam,
   I saw, upon a mossy bed
That wavered in the watery gloam,
   Where lay my lover drowned and dead.

Dead by my hand !   In my embrace
   I caught his cold form hard and close ;
And spurning back the water's race,
   Up to the outer air I rose.

And with all swiftness of my flight,
    Across the desolated plain
I bore him, lying still and white,
    Unto my cave beneath the main.

There as the 'reavèd lioness
    Moans, raging, o'er her stricken young,
Long days and nights my arms did press
    The dead, and on his neck I hung.

And all my sorceries I essayed,
    If haply some imperious spell
The gentle spirit might persuade
    Again in that fair form to dwell.

And many a fierce and forceful prayer
    Unto the gods I cried and said,
That for my service and despair
    They would but give me back my dead.

But every charm was all in vain;
    And to my prayers no answer came :
Only above the rippling main
    Murmured in mockery, aye the same.

At last, worn weary of my life
  For uselessness of prayer and spell,
I did forsake the empty strife
  'Gainst death ; and on the nymphs that dwell

In every coral-wroughten cave
  And every pearl and golden hall
That lies beneath the whirling wave,
  With one last effort I did call.

Then came they and with hallowing hands
  Bathed him in savours of the sea,
Wound his fair breast with silken bands
  Made potent with strange balsamry.

And many a sweet and secret verse
  And many a rude and antick rhyme—
Fraught with a spell—they did rehearse
  About the dead, that—till the time

When like the flaming of a scroll
  The heaven and earth shall pass away—
His perfect body fair and whole
  Should know no vestige of decay.

XII.

Since then, the gods have seized again
    Their full imperial sway on me :
For evermore, in heart and brain,
    I am their maid by land and sea :

I am their servant day and night
    To work on men their wrathful will,
To stand their champion in the fight
    Against the Nazarene, until

That unimaginable day,
    When in the throes of death and birth
The olden gods shall pass away ;
    When from the sea a new green earth

Shall rise, where in a glorious band,
    Transfigured and regenerate,
The new-born heavenly ones shall stand
    Before a new Valhalla's gate :

When I, content with ended strife,
    Shall with my glorious kindred die,
Haply to live with a new life
    In a new Asgard of the sky.

But lo ! the night draws on apace ;
  The sun is sunken in the west ;
And in the clouds meseems I trace
  The scarlet-burning Serpent's crest

Hurled up against the heaven.   The flame
  Of the gods' wrath burns up in me ;
And through my veins a searching shame
  Surges and will not set me free.

The maddening memory of my fall
  From the gods' service to the deep
Of woman's weakness, in the gall
  Of bitterness my soul doth steep.

And as I call back to my thought
  The time when I awhile resigned
Myself to love, my heart is wrought
  To rage, and wrath grips on my mind.

The bygone love for one man turns
  To hate against the world of men :
Within my soul the old fire burns,
  The thirst for ruin swells again.

6

Across the gathering gloom of sky
　　The dun clouds mass; and back and forth
See where the calling ravens fly
　　East unto west and south to north.

And lo! where in the sunset cloud,
　　Red as a sacrificial fire,
The form of Odin, thunder-browed,
　　Beckons unto my dread desire.

I know those signs: the old gods call
　　Upon their daughter to arise
From sloth, and on the storm-wind's spall,
　　To ride the tempest through the skies.

The thunder wakens: Odin nods,
　　And the sky blackens o'er the main:
My wings spread out: I come, great gods!
　　Your maid is wholly yours again!

Voices in the Air.

The soft skies darken ;
   The night draws near ;
I lie and hearken ;
   For in my ear
The land breeze rustles across the mere ;
The corby croons on the haunted brere.

The sea has shrouded
   The dying sun;
The air is clouded
   With mist-wreaths dun :
The gold lights flicker out one by one :
The day is ended, the night begun.

The pale stars glisten;
    The moon comes not:
I lie and listen
    I know not what:
Meseems the breath of the air is hot,
As though some levin across it shot.

    The petrels flutter
        Along the breeze:
    A moaning mutter
        Is on the seas:
A strange light over the billows flees;
The air is full of a vague unease.

    Alas, sweet sister,
        What fear draws nigh?
    What witch-lights glister
        Athwart the sky?
My heart with terror is like to die;
And some spell holds me: I cannot fly.

    Was that the thunder?
        A strange sound fled
    And fainted under
        The Westward red

My weak wings fail me for dint of dread ;
The silence weighs on my weary head.

O help me, sweetest !
Of all our race
Thou that art fleetest
And most of grace !
The dread of the night draws on apace,
And we are far from our resting-place.

Lo, there a levin !
From shore to shore
Of midmost heaven
Hell-bright it tore !
And hark, the thunder ! on heaven's floor
It breaks and volleys in roar on roar.

The witch ! She rises
Higher and higher !
The gleam of her eyes is
A blue bale-fire.
Her stern face surges ; her wings aspire ;
Her gold hair flames like a funeral pyre.

Her incantations
Are in the air :
From out their stations
On heaven's stair
The angels flutter in wild despair ;
The clouds catch fire at her floating hair.

Her spells have blotted
The stars from sight ;
The sea is clotted
With foam-wreaths white :
The storm-clouds shut out the heaven's light :
Hell's peoples gather across the night.

The sea grows higher,
And evermore
The storm draws nigher,
The billows roar :
The levins lighten us o'er and o'er ;
The fire-bolts hurtle on sea and shore.

Is there no fleeing ?
Sweet sister, speak.
Hearing and seeing
Grow dim and weak.

Is't grown too late and too far to seek
The land and the grot by the little creek?

I see death hover;
I cannot fly:
Is all hope over?
And must we die?
My voice is failing: I can but sigh:
Can this be death that is drawing nigh?

I call her vainly;
She answers not:
Alas! too plainly
The cause I wot.
Her sweet face sleeps in the dim sea-grot:
The sea snakes over her bosom knot.

The weed is clinging
Her locks among;
The sea is singing
Her wild death-song:
Farewell, sweet sister! but not for long:
Upon me also the death-chills throng.

The stern sea surges
Against the sky;
Like sobbing dirges
The wild winds sigh ;
My sea-drenched wings all powerless lie ;
The light is fading from heart and eye.

The billows thunder ;
The foam-bells flee :
My head sinks under
The raging sea :
The life is fainting, is failing me :
I come, sweet sister, I come to thee !

A BIRTHDAY SONG.

THE rose-time and the roses
  Call to me, dove of mine;
I hear the birdsong-closes
  Ring out in the sunshine;
In all the wood-reposes
  There runs a magic wine
  Of music all divine.

All things have scent and singing;
The happy earth is ringing
  With praise of love and June:
  Have I alone no tune,
No sound of music-making
To greet my love's awaking
  This golden summer noon?

II.

Ah, love ! my roses linger
  For sunshine of thine eyes ;
For Love the music-bringer,
  My linnets wait to rise ;
All dumb are birds and singer :
  The song in kisses dies
  And sound of happy sighs.

What need of songs and singing,
When love for us is ringing
  Bells of enchanted gold ?
  Dear, whilst my arms enfold
My love, our kisses fashion
Tunes of more perfect passion
  Than verses new or old.

VIRELAY.

A S I sate sorrowing,
   Love came and bade me sing
  A joyous song and meet :
For see (said he) each thing
Is merry for the Spring,
  And every bird doth greet
The break of blossoming,
That all the woodlands ring
  Unto the young hours' feet.

Wherefore put off defeat
And rouse thee to repeat
  The chime of merles that go,
With flutings shrill and sweet,
In every green retreat,

The tune of streams that flow
And mark the young hours' beat
With running ripples fleet
    And breezes soft and low.

For who should have, I trow,
Such joyance in the glow
    And pleasance of the May—
In all sweet bells that blow,
In death of winter's woe
    And birth of Springtide gay,
When in wood-walk and row
Hand-link'd the lovers go—
    As he to whom alway

God giveth, day by day,
To set to roundelay
    The sad and sunny hours—
To weave into a lay
Life's golden years and grey,
    Its sweet and bitter flowers—
To sweep, with hands that stray
In many a devious way,
    Its harp of sun and showers ?

Nor in this life of ours,
Whereon the sky oft lowers,
   Is any lovelier thing
Than in the wild wood bowers
The cloud of green that towers,
   The blithe birds welcoming
The vivid vernal hours
Among the painted flowers
   And all the pomp of Spring.

True, life is on the wing,
And all the birds that sing
   And all the flowers that be
Amid the glow and ring,
The pomp and glittering
   Of Spring's sweet pageantry,
Have here small sojourning;
And all our sweet hours bring
   Death nearer, as they flee.

Yet this thing learn of me:
The sweet hours fair and free
   That we have had of yore,
The fair things we did see,
The linkèd melody

Of waves upon the shore
That rippled in their glee,
Are not lost utterly,
    Though they return no more.

But in the true heart's core
Thought treasures evermore
    The tune of birds and breeze ;
And there the slow years store
The flowers our dead Springs wore
    And scent of blossomed leas ;
There murmurs o'er and o'er
The sound of woodlands hoar
    With newly burgeoned trees.

So for the sad soul's ease
Remembrance treasures these
    Against time's harvesting,
That so—when mild Death frees
The soul from Life's disease
    Of strife and sorrowing—
In glass of memories
The new hope looks and sees
    Through death a brighter Spring.

ALOE-BLOSSOM.

L IFE stayed for me within a breach of days,
      Sundered athwart the grey and rocky years :
   Above, the day was dim to me for fears
And memories of the many-chasmed ways
Through which my feet had struggled.   At amaze,
   Silent I stood and listened with wide ears,
   As for the coming of some Fate that nears
At last across the moon-mist and the haze.

The haggard earth lay speechless at my feet ;
   But as I waited, suddenly there came
   Within me as the flowering of a flame ;
And like the mystic bud that bursts to meet
   Its hundredth Spring with thunder and acclaim,
Love flowered upon me, terrible and sweet.

RONDEAU REDOUBLÉ.

MY day and night are in my lady's hand ;
    I have no other sunrise than her sight :
For me her favour glorifies the land ;
    Her anger darkens all the cheerful light,

    Her face is fairer than the hawthorn white,
When all a-flower in May the hedge-rows stand :
    Whilst she is kind, I know of none affright :
My day and night are in my lady's hand.

All heaven in her glorious eyes is spanned :
    Her smile is softer than the Summer night,
Gladder than daybreak on the Faery strand :
    I have no other sunrise than her sight.

    Her silver speech is like the singing flight
Of runnels rippling o'er the jewelled sand,
    Her kiss, a dream of delicate delight ;
For me her favour glorifies the land.

What if the Winter slay the Summer bland !
   The gold sun in her hair burns ever bright :
If she be sad, straightway all joy is banned ;
   Her anger darkens all the cheerful light.

Come weal or woe, I am my lady's knight
   And in her service every ill withstand :
Love is my lord, in all the world's despite,
   And holdeth in the hollow of his hand
      My day and night.

AZIZEH'S TOMB.

I PASSED by a ruined tomb in the midst of a
garden-way, Upon whose letterless stone
seven blood-red anemones lay.

"Who sleeps in this unmarked grave?" I said; and
the earth, "Bend low; For a lover lies here
and waits for the Resurrection Day."

"God keep thee, O victim of love!" I cried, "and
bring thee to dwell In the highest of all the
heavens of Paradise, I pray!

"How wretched are lovers all, even in the sepulchre,
For their very tombs are covered with ruin
and decay!

"Lo! if I might, I would plant thee a garden round
about, And with my streaming tears the thirst
of its flowers allay!"

From the Arabic.

DREAM-LIFE.

IT seems to me sometimes that I am dead
   And watch the live world in its ceaseless stream
   Pass by me through the pauses of a dream.
The dawn breaks blue on them, the sunset's red
Burns on their smiles and on the tears they shed ;
   The moonlight floods them with its silver gleam :
   To me they are as ghosts that do but seem ;
Their grief is strange to me, their gladness dread.

Life lapses, like a vision dim and grey,
   Before my sight, a cloud-wrack in the sky :
   Since I am dead I can no longer die :
   Ah, can it be this doom is laid on me,
To see the tired world slowly pass away,
   Nor die, but live on everlastingly ?

SONNET.

CHIDE me who will for that my song is sad,
    And all my fancy follows on the wave
   That bears our little being to the grave !
When did it fail that those—whose lives were glad
For lack of light and want of virtue had
    To know the mystery and the hair-hung glaive
   That shadow all our life so seeming brave—
The accusing wail of those that weep forbad ?

Peace, triflers ! Peace, dull ears and heedless eyne !
    Yet haply Time unto your foolish fears
   Shall yield a mocking áccord, and the years,
Falling full-fated on these days of mine,
Crush from the grapes of grief a bitter wine
   Of laughters, sadder than the saddest tears.

THE BALLAD OF ISOBEL.

THE BALLAD OF ISOBEL.

I.

THE day is dead, the night draws on,
  The shadows gather fast :
'Tis many an hour yet to the dawn,
  Till Hallow-tide be past.

Till Hallow-tide be past and sped,
  The night is full of fear ;
For then they say the restless dead
  Unto the live draw near.

Between the Saints' day and the Souls'
  The dead wake in the mould ;
The poor dead, in their grassy knolls
  They lie and are a-cold.

They think upon the live that sit
  And drink the Hallow-ale,
Whilst they lie stark within the pit,
  Nailed down with many a nail.

And sore they wonder if the thought
  Live in them of the dead ;
And sore with wish they are distraught
  To feel the firelight red.

Betwixt the day and yet the day
  The Saints' and Souls' divide,
The dead folk rise out of the clay
  And wander far and wide.

They wander o'er the sheeted snow,
  Chill with the frore of death,
Until they see the windows glow
  With the fire's ruddy breath.

And if the cottage door be fast
  And but the light win out,
All night, until their hour is past,
  The dead walk thereabout.

And all night long, the live folk hear
  Their windy song of sighs,
And waken all for very fear,
  Until the white day rise.

But if the folk be piteous
 And pity the poor dead
That weary in the narrow house,
 Upon the cold earth's bed,

They pile the peats upon the fire
 And leave the door ajar,
That so the rosy flame aspire
 To where the grey ghosts are.

And syne they sweep the cottage floor
 And set the hearthside chair :
The sad dead watch beside the door,
 Till midnight still the air.

And then towards the friendly glow
 Come trooping in the dead ;
Until the cocks for morning crow,
 They sit by the fire red.

II.

" Oh, I have wearied long enough !
 I'll weary me no more ;
But I will watch for my dead love
 Till Hallow-tide be o'er."

He set the door across the sill ;
   The moonlight fluttered in :
The sad snow covered heath and hill,
   As far as eye could win.

The thin frost feathered in the air ;
   All dumb the white world lay ;
Night sat on it as cold and fair
   As death upon a may.

He turned him back into the room
   And sat him by the fire :
Night darkened round him in the gloom
   The shadowtide rose higher.

He rose and looked out o'er the hill
   To where the grey kirk lay ;
The midnight quiet was so still,
   He heard the bell-chimes play.

Twelve times he heard the sweet bell chime ;
   No whit he stirred or spoke ;
But his eyes fixed, as if on Time
   The hour of judgment broke.

And as the last stroke fell and died,
  Over the kirkyard grey
Himseemed he saw a blue flame glide,
  Among the graves at play.

A flutter waved upon the breeze
  As of a spirit's wings :
A wind went by him through the trees,
  That spoke of heavenly things.

Himseemed he heard a sound of feet
  Upon the silver snow :
A rush of robes by him did fleet,
  A sighing soft and low.

He turned and sat him down again ;
  The midnight filled the place :
The tears ran down like silent rain
  Upon his weary face.

"She will not come to me," he said ;
  "The death-swoon is too strong :
She hath forgot me with the dead,
  Me that she loved so long.

"She will not come : she sleeps too sweet
    Within the quiet ground.
What worth is love, when life is fleet
    And sleep in death so sound?

"She will not come !"—A soft cold air
    Upon his forehead fell :
He turned him to the empty chair ;
    And there sat Isobel.

His dead love sat him side by side,
    His minnie white and wan :
Within the tomb she could not bide,
    Whilst he sat weeping on.

Ah, wasted, wasted was her face
    And sore her cheek was white :
But in her eyes the ancient grace
    Burnt with a feeble light.

Upon her breast the grave-weed grey
    Fell to her little feet :
But still the golden tresses lay
    About her bosom sweet.

" Ah, how is't with ye, Isobel ?
    How pale ye look and cold !
Ah, sore it is to think ye dwell
    Alone beneath the mould !

" Is't weary for our love ye've grown
    From dwelling with the dead,
Or shivering from the cold grave-stone
    To find the firelight red ?"

" Oh, 'tis not that I'm lorn of love
    Or that a-cold I lie :
I trust in God that is above
    To bring you by-and-bye.

" I feel your kisses on my face,
    Your kisses sweet and warm :
Your love is in the burial-place ;
    I fear nor cold nor worm.

" I feel the love within your heart
    That beats for me alone :
I fear not change upon your part
    Nor crave for the unknown.

" For to the dead no faint fears cling :
 All certainty have they :
They know (and smile at sorrowing)
 Love never dies away.

" No harm can reach me in Death's deep:
 It hath no fear for me :
God sweetens it to lie and sleep,
 Until His face I see :

" He makes it sweet to lie and wait,
 Till we together meet
And hand-in-hand athwart the gate
 Pass up the golden street. ,

" But where's the babe that at my side
 Slept sweetly long ago ?
So sore to me to-night it cried,
 I could not choose but go.

" I heard its voice so full of wail,
 It woke me in the grave :
Its sighs came to me on the gale,
 Across the wintry wave.

" For though death lap her wide and mild,
   A mother cannot rest,
Except her little sucking child
   Be sleeping at her breast."

" Ah, know'st thou not, my love ?" he said :
   " Methought the dead knew all.
When in that night of doom and dread
   The moving waters' wall

" Smote on our ship and drove it down
   Beneath the raging sea,
All of our company did drown,
   Alas ! save only me.

" And me the cruel billows cast
   Aswoon upon the strand ;
Thou dead within my arms held fast,
   Hand locked in other's hand.

" The ocean never to this day
   Gave up our baby dead :
Ah, woe is me that life should stay,
   When all its sweet is fled !"

" Go down," said she, " to the seashore :
  God taketh ruth on thee :
Search well ; and I will come once more
  Ere yet the midnight be."

She bent her sweet pale mouth to his :
  The snowdrift from the sky
Falls not so cold as did that kiss :
  He shook as he should die.

She looked on him with yearning eyes
  And vanished from his sight :
He heard the matin cock crow thrice ;
  The morning glimmered white.

III.

Then from his place he rose and sought
  The shore beside the sea :
And there all day he searched ; but nought
  Until the eve found he.

At last a pale star glittered through
  The growing dusk of night,
And fell upon the waste of blue,
  A trembling wand of light.

And lo ! a wondrous thing befell :
    As though the small star's ray
Availed to break some year-old spell
    That on the water lay.

A white form rose out of the deep
    Where it so long had lain,
Cradled within the cold death-sleep :
    He knew his babe again.

It floated softly to his feet ;
    White as a flower it lay :
God's love had kept its body sweet
    Unravished óf decay.

He thanked God weeping for His grace ;
    And many a tear he shed
And many a kiss upon its face
    That smiled as do the dead.

Then to the kirkyard where the maid
    Slept cold in clay he hied ;
And with a loving hand he laid
    The baby by her side.

IV.

The dark fell down upon the earth ;
  Night held the quiet air :
He sat before the glowing hearth,
  Beside the empty chair.

Twelve times at last for middle night
  Rang out the kirkyard bell :
Ere yet the twelfth was silent quite,
  By him sat Isobel.

Within her arms their little child
  Lay pillowed on her breast :
Death seemed to it as soft and mild
  As heaven to the blest.

Ah, no more wasted was her face,
  Nor white her cheek and wan !
The splendour of a heavenly grace
  Upon her forehead shone.

She seemed again the golden girl
  Of the long-vanished years :
Her face shone as a great sweet pearl,
  Washed and made white in tears.

The light of heaven filled her eyes
  With soft and splendid flame ;
Out of the heart of Paradise
  It seemed as if she came.

He looked upon her beauty bright ;
  And sore, sore weepit he,
To think how many a day and night
  Between them yet must be.

He looked at her with many a sigh ;
  For sick he was with pain,
To think how many a year must fly
  Ere they two met again.

She looked on him : no sadness lay
  Upon her tender mouth ;
And syne she smiled, a smile as gay
  And glad as in her youth.

" Be of good cheer, dear heart," said she :
  " Yet but a little year
Ere thou and I together see
  The end of doubt and fear.

"Come once again the saints' night ring
   Unto the spirits' feet,
Glad with the end of sorrowing,
   Once more we three shall meet :

"We three shall meet no more to part
   For all eternity ;
'Gin I come not to thee, sweetheart,
   Do thou come then to me."

V.

Another year is past and gone :
   Once more the lingering light
Fades from the sky, and dusk falls down
   Upon the Holy Night.

The hearth is clear ; the fire burns red ;
   The door stands open wide :
He waits for the belovèd dead
   To come with Hallow-tide.

The midnight rings out loud and slow
   Across the frosty air :
He sits before the firelight-glow,
   Beside the waiting chair.

The last chime dies into the night :
   The stillness grows apace :
And yet there comes no lady bright
   To fill the empty place.

No soft hand falls upon his hair ;
   No light breath fans his brow :
The night is empty everywhere ;
   The birds sleep on the bough.

" Ah woe is me ! the night fades fast ;
   Her promise is forgot :
Alas !" he said, " the hours fly past,
   And still she cometh not !

" So sweet she sleeps, and sleeps with her
   The baby at her breast,
No thought of earthly love can stir
   Their undesireful rest.

" Ah, who can tell but Time may lay
   Betwixt us such a space
That haply at the Judgment Day
   She will forget my face."

The still night quivered as he spoke ;
    He felt the midnight air :
Throb, and a little breeze awoke
    Across the heather bare.

And in the wind himseemed he heard
    His true love's voice once more :
Afar it came, and but one word
    " Come !" unto him it bore.

A faint hope flickered in his breast :
    He rose and took his way
Where underneath the brown hill's crest
    The quiet kirkyard lay.

He pushed the lychgate to the wall :
    Against the moonless sky
The grey kirk towered dusk and tall :
    Heaven seemed on it to lie.

Dead darkness held the holy ground ;
    His feet went in and out
And stumbled at each grassy mound,
    As one that is in doubt.

Then suddenly the sky grew white;
  The moon thrust through the gloom :
The tall tower's shade against her light
  Fell on his minnie's tomb.

Full on her grave its shadow fell,
  As 'twere a giant's hand,
That motionless the way doth tell
  Unto the heavenly land.

He fell upon his knees thereby
  And kissed the holy earth,
Wherein the only twain did lie
  That made life living-worth.

He knelt ; no longer did he weep ;
  Great peace was on his soul :
Sleep sank on him, a wondrous sleep,
  Assaining death and dole.

And in the sleep himseemed he stood
  Before a high gold door,
Upon whose midst the blessèd Rood
  Burnt like an opal's core.

Christ shining on the cross to see
  Was there for all device :
Within he saw the almond-tree
  That grows in Paradise.

He knew the fallen almond-flowers
  That drop without the gate,
So with their scent the tardy hours
  Be cheered for those that wait.

And as he looked, a glimmering light
  Shone through the blazoned bars :
The wide tall gate grew blue and bright
  As Heaven with the stars.

A postern opened in his face ;
  Sweet savours breathed about ;
And through the little open space
  A fair white hand came out :

A hand as white as ermolin,
  A hand he knew full well,
Beckoned to him to enter in—
  The hand of Isobel.

Lord Christ, Thy morning tarrieth long :
 The shadows come and go :
These three have heard the angels' song :
 Still many wait below.

These three on Heaven's honey feed,
 And milk of Paradise :
How long before for us indeed
 The hills of Heaven rise?

How long before, joined hand-in-hand
 With all the dear loved dead,
We pass along the heavenly land
 And hear the angels' tread ?

The night is long : the way is drear :
 Our hearts faint for the light :
Vouchsafe, Lord Christ, the day draw near,
 The morning of Thy sight !

INDIAN SUMMER.

I.

I SAID "The time of grief is overpast :
The mists of morning hold the plains no more :
The flowers of Spring are dead ; the woods that
wore
The silver suits of Summer o'er them cast
Are stripped and bare before the wintry blast.
Is it for thee to weary and implore
The ruthless Gods, to beat against their door
For ever and for ever to the last ?
Rise and be strong—yonder the new life lies.
Who knows but haply, past the sand-hills traced
Bounding the prospect, Destiny have placed
A sunny land of flowers and sapphire skies,
For balm of hearts and cure of loves laid waste ?
Up, and leave weeping to a woman's eyes !"

II.

Then turned I sadly to the olden signs
    By which I had so long lived lingering ;
    The faded woods, the birds long ceased to sing
And the dead grapes dried on the withered vines,
And the thin rill that through the time-worn lines
    Of grey-leaved herbs fled faintly murmuring
    Its ghostly memories of the songs of Spring,
Weird whispers of the wind among the pines.
Farewell I bade them all, with heart as sad
    Well-nigh as when Love left me long ago,
And turned into the distance.   Long I had
    Their murmur in my ears, as long and slow
The melancholy way did spread and wind
That left the memories of youth behind.

III.

At last a new land opened on my view :
    No phantom of the dear dead Spring of old
    It was, but a fair land of Autumn gold
And corn-fields sloping to a sea of blue :
And I looked down upon its face and knew
    The Autumn land of which my heart had told,
    The land where Love at last should be consoled

And balm flower forth among Life's leaves of rue.
A sunset-land it was; and long and sweet,
   The shadows of the setting lay on it :
   And through the long fair valleys there did flit
Strange birds with pale gold wings, that did repeat
   The loveliest songs whereof men aye had wit ;
   And over all the legend " Peace " was writ.

IV.

And as I gazed on it, my heart was filled
   With rapture of the sudden cease of pain :
   And in my spirit, ever and again,
There rang the golden legend, sweet and stilled
With speech of birds ; and in the pauses rilled
   Fair fountains through the green peace of the plain,
   That with the tinkle of their golden rain
Made carol to the songs the linnets trilled :
Whilst, over all, the waves upon the shore
   Throbbed with a music, sad but very sweet,
That had in it the melodies of yore,
   Softened, as when the angels do repeat,
In heaven, to souls in rapture of new birth,
The names that they have sadly borne on earth.

LOVE'S AMULET.

SONG, be strong and true to hold
  Love within thy locks of gold :
Bind my lady's thought with rhyme ;
Kiss her if her lips grow cold ;
Bring her thoughts of Summer-prime,
Lest her heart catch winter-time.
    Song, be quick and bold.

  Take her flowers of love and light,
Blossoms of her soul's delight,
Roses of her heart's desire ;
Bind her brow with lilies white ;
Lilies' snow and roses' fire
Hold love's summer ever by her,
    In the world's despite.

  Strew the Springtime in her way,
Lest she weary of the day,

Lest the lonely hours be long ;
Be her season ever May,
May, when Love is safe from wrong
And with larks' and linnets' song
   All the world is gay.

   Sweet, I wind thee with a chain,
Verses linked in one refrain,
" Love me, love, who love but thee,"
Piping ever and again ;
Bind thy thought and heart to be
Constant aye to Love and me
   Thorow joy and pain.

DOUBLE BALLAD

Of the Singers of the Time.

I.

WHY are our songs like the moan of the main,
    When the wild winds buffet it to and fro,
(Our brothers ask us again and again)
    A weary burden of hopes laid low?
    Have birds ceased singing or flowers to blow?
Is Life cast down from its fair estate?
    This I answer them—nothing mo'—
Songs and singers are out of date.

II.

What shall we sing of? Our hearts are fain.
    Our bosoms burn with a sterile glow.
Shall we sing of the sordid strife for gain,
    For shameful honour, for wealth and woe,

Hunger and luxury,—weeds that throw
Up from one seeding their flowers of hate?
  Can we tune our lutes to these themes? Ah no!
Songs and singers are out of date.

III.

Our songs should be of Faith without stain,
  Of haughty honour and deaths that sow
The seeds of life on the battle-plain,
  Of loves unsullied and eyes that show
  'The fair white soul in the deeps below.
Where are they, these that our songs await
  To wake to joyance?   Doth any know?
Songs and singers are out of date.

IV.

What have we done with meadow and lane?
  Where are the flowers and the hawthorn-snow?
Acres of brick in the pitiless rain,—
  These are our gardens for thorpe and stow!
  Summer has left us long ago,
Gone to the lands where the turtles mate
  And the crickets chirp in the wild-rose row.
Songs and singers are out of date.

V.

We sit and sing to a world in pain ;
  Our heartstrings quiver sadly and slow :
But, aye and anon, the murmurous strain
    Swells up to a clangour of strife and throe,
    And the folk that hearken, or friend or foe,
Are ware that the stress of the time is great
    And say to themselves, as they come and go,
Songs and singers are out of date.

VI.

Winter holds us, body and brain :
  Ice is over our being's flow ;
Song is a flower that will droop and wane,
    If it have no heaven towards which to grow.
    Faith and beauty are dead, I trow
Nothing is left but fear and fate :
    Men are weary of hope ; and so
Songs and singers are out of date.

MADRIGAL GAI.

THE summer-sunshine comes and goes ;
   The bee hums in the heart of the rose :
   Heart of my hope, the year is sweet ;
   The lilies lighten about thy feet.

A new light glitters on land and sea ;
   The turtles couple on every tree.
   Light of my life, the fields are fair ;
   Gossamers tangle thy golden hair.

The air with kisses is blithe and gay ;
   Love is so sweet in the middle May.
   Sweet of my soul, the brook is blue ;
   Thine eyes with heaven have pierced it through.

Now is the time for kisses, now
   When bird-songs babble from every bough !
   Sweetest, my soul is a bird that sips
   Honey of heaven from out thy lips.

BALLAD OF POETS.

WHAT do we here, who with reverted eyes
  Turn back our longings from the modern air
To the dim gold of long-evanished skies,
When other songs in other mouths were fair?
Why do we stay the load of life to bear,
To measure still the weary worldly ways,
Waiting upon the still-recurring sun,
That ushers in another waste of days,
Of roseless Junes and unenchanted Mays—
Why but because our task is yet undone ?

  Were it not thus, could but our high emprize
Be once fulfilled, which of us would forbear
To seek that haven where contentment lies?
Who would not doff at once life's load of care,
To sleep at peace amid the silence there ?

9—2

Ah, who alas ?—Across the heat and haze,
Death beckons to us in the shadow dun,
Favouring and fair—" My rest is sweet," he says :
But we reluctantly avert our gaze ;
Why but because our task is yet undone ?

III.

Songs have we sung, and many melodies
Have from our lips had issue rich and rare :
But never yet the conquering chant did rise,
That should ascend the very heaven's stair,
To rescue life from anguish and despair.
Often and again, drunk with delight of lays,
" Lo," have we cried, " this is the golden one
That shall deliver us !"—Alas ! Hope's rays
Die in the distance, and life's sadness stays :
Why but because our task is yet undone ?

Envoi.

Great God of Love, thou whom all poets praise,
Grant that the aim of rest for us be won !
Let the light shine upon our life that strays,
Disconsolate, within the desert maze,
Why but because our task is yet undone ?

FADED LOVE.

*FAREWELL, sweetheart: Farewell, our golden
days!*
So runs the cadence, ringing out the tune
Of sighs and kisses : for the tale of June
Is told, and all the length of flowered ways
Fades in the distance, as the new life lays
Its hand upon the strings, and all too soon
Breaks the brief song of birds and flowers and
moon
That held the Maytime—what is this that stays ?
--A white-robed figure, with sad eyes that hold
A far-off dream of never-travelled ways,—
Wan with white lips and hands as pale and cold
As woven garlands of long vanished Mays,
And the sun's memory halo-like above
Its head?—It is the thought of faded Love.

VILLANELLE.

THE air is white with snow-flakes clinging ;
    Between the gusts that come and go
Methinks I hear the woodlark singing.

    Methinks I see the primrose springing
On many a bank and hedge, although
The air is white with snowflakes clinging.

    Surely, the hands of Spring are flinging
Wood-scents to all the winds that blow :
Methinks I hear the woodlark singing.

    Methinks I see the swallow winging
Across the woodlands sad with snow ;
The air is white with snowflakes clinging.

    Was that the cuckoo's wood-chime swinging ?
Was that the linnet fluting low ?
Methinks I hear the woodlark singing.

Or can it be the breeze is bringing
The breath of violets? Ah no!
The air is white with snowflakes clinging.

It is my lady's voice that's stringing
Its beads of gold to song; and so
Methinks I hear the woodlark singing.

The violets I see upspringing
Are in my lady's eyes, I trow :
The air is white with snowflakes clinging.

Dear, whilst thy tender tones are ringing,
Even whilst amidst the winter's woe
The air is white with snowflakes clinging,
Methinks I hear the woodlark singing.

RITOURNEL.

O CENSOR of Love! Thou that art bright as
the day,
Fortunate, clad with delight as the trees in May
If Fate with its cruel hand should thee assay,
Then wilt thou taste of its bitter cup and say,
Alas for Love and out on his whole array !
My heart with his flaming fires is burnt away.

But to-day thou art safe as yet from his fell com-
mands,
And his perfidy holds thee not in its iron bands ;
So scoff not at those that languish beneath his hands
And cry, for excess of passion that doth them slay,
Alas for Love and out on his whole array !
My heart with his flaming fires is burnt away.

Be not of those that look on Love with disdain,
But rather excuse and pity the lover's pain,
Lest thou be bound one day in the self-same chain,
And drink of the self-same bitter draught as they.
Alas for Love and out on his whole array !
My heart with his flaming fires is burnt away.

There is none that can tell of Love and its bitter
ness
But he that is sick and weak for its long excess,
He who has lost his reason for love-distress,
Whose drink is the bitter dregs of his own dismay.
Alas for Love and out on his whole array !
My heart with his flaming fires is burnt away.

How many a lover watches the darksome night,
His eyes forbidden the taste of sleep's delight!
How many whose tears, like rivers adown a height,
Course down their cheeks ! How many are they that
say,
Alas for Love and out on his whole array !
My heart with his flaming fires is burnt away.

How many a lover wasteth for sheer despair,
Wakeful, for void of sleep is the dusky air !
Languor and pain are the clothes that he doth wear,

And even his pleasant dreams have gone astray.
Alas for Love and out on his whole array !
My heart with his flaming fires is burnt away.

I too of old was empty of heart and free
And lay down to rest in peace till I met with thee :
The taste of the sleepless nights was strange to me
Till Love did beckon and I must needs obey,
Alas for Love and out on his whole array !
My heart with his flaming fires is burnt away.

How often my patience fails and my bones do
   waste,
And my tears, like a fount of blood, stream down in
   haste !
For my life, that of old was pleasant and sweet of
   taste,
A slender maiden hath bittered this many a day.
Alas for Love and out on his whole array !
My heart with his flaming fires is burnt away.

Alack for the man among men that loves like me
And watches the wings of the night through the
   shadows flee !
Who drowns in his own despair as it were a sea,

Who cries in the stress of an anguish without allay,
Alas for Love and out on his whole array !
My heart with his flaming fires is burnt away.

Whom hath not Love stricken and wounded
indeed ?
Who has been aye from his easy fetters freed ?
Whose life is empty of Love, and who succeed
In winning their hearts' delight without affray ?
Alas for Love and out on his whole array !
My heart with his flaming fires is burnt away.

From the Arabic.

RONDEL.

K ISS me, sweetheart, the Spring is here,
   And Love is lord of you and me!
The bluebells beckon each passing bee;
The wild wood laughs to the flowered year:
There is no bird in brake or brere
   But to his little mate sings he,
" Kiss me, sweetheart, the Spring is here,
   And Love is lord of you and me."

The blue sky laughs out sweet and clear;
   The missel-thrush upon the tree
   Pipes for sheer gladness loud and free;
And I go singing to my dear,
" Kiss me, sweetheart, the Spring is here,
   And Love is lord of you and me!"

LIGHT O' LOVE.

LIGHT O' LOVE.

WE dwelt within a wood of thought,
    I and my days ; and no man sought
Or cared to comfort us in aught.

    A strange sad company we were,
Calm with the quiet of despair,
As sunset in the autumn air.

    No thing we had, nor cared to win,
Of all for which men toil or spin :
We took no kind of joy therein.

    Nor any glimpse to us was given
Of that wherefor we once had striven,
The love that likens earth with heaven.

But some strange spell was wound about
Our lives, a charm of hope and doubt,
That severed us from lives without ;

A charm that was not weft of flowers
Of night alone or winter hours—
This binding gramarye of ours,—

But grew of delicate sweet blooms
That, found of old in woodland glooms,
Had drawn us from the waste world-rooms

To seek the singing solitudes,
Where some unforced enchantment broods,
And never any foot intrudes.

And drinking deep of dews that fell
And sparkled in some woodflower's bell,
Made potent with a drowsy spell,

The charm on us had taken hold,
And like a mist about us rolled,
The pale dreams wavered white and cold.

A mist of charms that spread between
Us and the world, so that, I ween,
We were not heard of men or seen.

But folk passed by and knew us not :
And day by day, the fatal lot
A stronger grasp upon us got.

Until the sighs and tears we spent
About us for bewilderment
Did fructify, and earth was sprent

Around us with a flush of flower
Sad-hued ; and tall dusk trees did tower
And clung about us like a bower.

So that, one day, when we awoke,
I and my days, and would have broke
The dream and let the gold sun-stroke

Into our lives, the outward way
Was set with hawthorns white and grey
And trees that shouldered back the day.

And from the world of men there came
Nor sound of bell nor sight of flame,
And no man called us by our name.

But outerward we heard the roll
Of daily life through joy and dole
And pleasant labour ; but no soul

Strayed from the highway or the mart
To where within the wild wood-heart
I and my days we sat apart.

Then to my days I said, " Behold,
The memory of our life is cold,
And no man knows us as of old.

"Shall we go forth and seek for grace ?
Lo, men have all forgot our face !
Another sitteth in our place.

" Let us sit down again, my days,
Here where our dreams have built a maze
Of flowers for us and woodland ways.

" For of a surety no thing
Shall profit us of sorrowing,
Nor strife can comfort to us bring.

" Here will we sit and let the sweep
Of life roll by : in this wood-deep,
Our dreams shall carol us to sleep."

Then in that pleasant woodland-shade,
I and my days full fain we made
A dwelling-place, and therein stayed.

Most fair that forest was, and full
Of birds and all things beautiful ;
And many a pleasant green-set pool

Was there, where fawns came down to drink
At eventide : and on the brink
The nodding cuckoo-bells did blink.

By one of these, thick-bowered among
A nest of hawthorns, all a-throng
With birds that filled the air with song,

We builded us a dwelling-place,
Set in a little sun-screened space,
Midmost the forest's dreamy grace.

And there full many a day we spent,
Lost in a dream of dim content,
I and my days, what while there went

Without the many-coloured hours,
Golden or sad.   With flush of flowers
We calendared this life of ours.

For many a precious thing and fair
We had heaped up and garnered there,
And many a jewel bright and rare ;

And of a truth our hands were full
Of memories most beautiful,
And dreams whose glitterance did dull

Remembered sunlight in our thought :
So rich we were, that memory brought
No yearning for the world in aught.

And too, each one of these my days
Had, wandering in the wild wood-ways,
Caught from the birds some note of lays

More sweet than waking ears can deem
Or in the mazes of the dream
Had found some gem of all that teem

Within the mystery of thought,
Some pearl of hidden arts, or caught
Some strange sweet secret, all inwrought

With scent of leaves and forest-flowers
And glitter of enchanted showers
Fallen athwart the sunset-towers.

And all the wonders of the wood,
And all the pleasance that did brood
Within that silver solitude,

Jewelled with cups of gold and blue
And veined with waters cleaving through
The live green of the leafage new,

Some one of these could bring to sight.
One led to where, like living light,
The clearest thread of streams took flight

Across the mosses, and could tell
The hour when on the water fell
The shadow of some mystic spell

That called the hidden nymphs to sight,
And from the dell-deeps, in the night,
The wood-girls flashed out, tall and white,

Across the moonbeams ; or the time,
When through the birds' sunsetting chime
The glades rang with the tinkling rhyme

Of the wild wood-folk : and one knew
Where such a flush of violets grew,
That therewithal the earth was blue.

And yet another one could show
The wood-nooks where the blue-bells blow,
And banks are sweet with lily-snow.

And one had heard the wild bird sing—
In some dim close, where in a ring
The apple-trees together cling—

So sweet a song, it seemed the breath
Of souls that know not life nor death,
In fields where Heaven's Spring flowereth.

And one, the youngest of them all,
Had heard the elf-dance rise and fall,
Where with the moon the woodbind-wall

Shines silver in the wood-glooms deep :
And one had seen the white nix leap,
When the blue water lay asleep.

And one had caught the mystic tune
The sea sings underneath the moon,
When earth with Summer lies aswoon.

And one had lit by fairy grace,
Wandering afield, upon a place
Where, if a man shall lie a space

And slumber in the flower swaths dim,
The sweet dreams whisper love to him,
Till night burns dawn-red at the rim.

And yet another, wandering,
Had found the caves where rubies cling
To earth, and many a precious thing

Of jewelries burns manifold
Within the darkness, and the mould
Is spangled with the dust of gold.

And some had trod the secret ways
Where in the dusk the sun's lost rays
Harden into the diamond's blaze;

And threading through the hill-caves brown,
Had lit upon vast chambers, strown
With coloured crystals,—and had known

The silver splendours of the caves
That run out underneath the waves,
Walled with thick pearl and hung with glaives

Of branching coral,—and the maze
Of all the golden sweet sea-ways,
Where, jewel-like, the thin light strays

On golden fish and pearléd sand,
And like a wood, on either hand,
The waving banks of seaweed stand.

And others of the band could tell
Tales of the lands delectable,
Upon whose glory, like a spell,

The splendour of the unknown lies ;
Stories of Ind and Orient skies,
Of far East isles where never dies

The golden noonlight quite away,
But night is like a silver day ;
And of vast cities, which men say

Gods built ; or that sweet Syrian stead,
The city rose-engarlanded,
Girdled with many a silver thread

Of rivers running sweet and wild
Through gardens tamarisk-enisled
And orange-groves with blossom piled ;

Or that clear Paradise that stands,
Builded of old by giant hands,
Invisible among the sands

Of those enchanted plains of Fars,
Where from the East narcissus-stars
Spread white towards the sunset-bars ;

And stories of the strange sweet lands
Where, like a tower, the tulip stands
And jasmines through the wood link hands ;

Where curtain-like the mosses fall,
Silver, athwart the banyan-hall,
And in the night the wild swans call ;

And of the clear-eyed lakes that shine
Bright as the laughing heart of wine,
Alive with flower-hued snakes that twine

Round mystic flowers therein that are,
Blue lotus and gold nenuphar
And many a silver lily-star.

These all they knew, and many a thing
Yet lovelier in remembering :
And eke full many an one could sing

Such soul-sweet songs, the very deer
Came down at eventide to hear :
And as they rang out soft and clear,

The singing echoes of the wood
Woke up out of their silent mood,
And with full tones the strains pursued

Through all the lengthening cells of sound,
And all the trees that stood around
Waved to the rhythm, music-bound.

Some clarion-shrill, some softliest
Did sing ; and some sighed as the west
Sighs to the night ; but in my breast

A nest of singing birds I had,
Whose song was sweet, but very sad ;
And yet by times it made me glad.

And these, past all, I loved to hear,
What time they fluted, low and clear,
Soft songs that did caress my ear

With memories of a Paradise,
That ne'er before my weary eyes
Had risen, nor should ever rise

Till Death (mayhap) should set the gate
Open for me, and I, elate,
See all my hopes for me await.

And sometimes many a weary day
The birds within my bosom lay
Voiceless and still.　And then full grey

And sick my life was even to death ;
Till, with a swift and sudden breath
Of impulse, as of some sweet faith

New risen, all the silence fled,
The voices rose up from the dead,
And with one gush of music spread

New waves of peace through all my soul ;
And then my life put off its dole,
And of my grief I was made whole.

So many days this life we led,
Curtained with solitudes and fed
With drink of dreams ; and as the dead

Hear afar off, with listless ears,
The hurry of the outer years,
But sleep, absolved of doubts and fears,

So unto us sometimes would come
An echo of the worldly hum,
Breaking our silence spirit-dumb,

And stirred our thought to memories
Of earthly passion : but, like sighs
Of some vague melody that dies .

If one give heed unto its strain,
The distant hum did faint and wane ;
And peace encurtained us again.

For all our life was filled and sweet
With fair glad dreams ; and every beat
Of the clear-echoing hours did greet

Our sense with some new ravishment
Of thoughts and fancies : and a scent
Of mystic unseen flowers was blent

For ever with our daily air,
As if some angel, hovering near,
Shook odours from his floating hair.

And thus our days went by for long,
Filled with the glory of a song ;
And not a touch of care did wrong

The eternal Springtide of our dream,
And not a ripple broke the gleam
That slept along our life's full stream.

But as the years went on and on,
All gradually our lives grew wan
With some vague yearning ; and there shone,

Day after day, less gloriously
The softened splendour in the sky ;
And one by one, the lights did die

Within our spirit.   Day by day,
Less joy we took in all that lay
Of beauty in wood-dell or way ;

And the heaped jewels in the shade
Of our new gloom did change and fade
And waste before our eyes dismayed.

And no more did we love to go
About the woodlands, in the glow
Of noonday, or to watch the flow

Of rillets through the flower-ringed grass,
Or see the dappled shadows pass
Across the lake's full-lilied glass.

But all our early joys seemed dead
And colourless to us : like lead,
Upon our lives the stillness weighed.

The ringdove's voice and every note
The wild lark shook out from his throat
And all the linnet's music smote

Upon our senses like a knell ;
And day by day, a sterner spell
Of hopeless yearning on us fell.

And each fair thing, that we had won
In times bygone, did seem fordone
Of all its loveliness : and none

Of all my days had aught of price
Or any delicate device,
Could cheer them ; but the cruel ice

Of death seemed on them all to lie,
And all their dainty lore laid by ;
So that they saw with careless eye

The secret things they loved so well,
And wandered on through wood and dell,
Careless of aught to them befell.

And some, on treasure having lit,
Had dug a grave and buried it,
So that it gladdened them no whit.

And now each sound of toil or sport,
That reached our weary ears athwart
The wood-screens of our forest-court,

Maddened our yearning : and full fain
We grew towards the world again ;
And gladly would we now have ta'en

The olden burdens : but the way
Was shut with tangled woods that lay
And closed each exit to the day.

And oftentimes, our weary feet
Did wander from the wood-deeps sweet,
Green-golden in the noontide heat,

Into a little path, that led,
Through tangling hawthorns blossom-spread,
To where sea-cliffs rose white and red

Above a many-coloured beach ;
And through a rugged mountain-breach,
We came to where the sea did reach

Into the golden-margined sky :
And there wide ripples came to die
Upon the sands, with one long sigh

So sad and so monotonous,
In very sooth it seemed to us
It was our own grief rendered thus.

And there we loved to sit and hear
The long waves murmur in our ear,
And watch the ripples low and clear

Lengthen across the swelling tide :
And now and then our eyes espied
A distant snowy glimmer glide

Along the sky-line, as it were
Some white-sailed vessel that did fare
Towards the shore.   But never near

The vision drew : and wearily
We watched the glimmer fade and flee,
Then turned our footsteps from the sea.

But yet, a spark of old delight
Gladdened us sometimes ; and the light
Slid over all and made life bright

By times awhile : for in my breast
The songbirds sang out from their nest
Sweetlier than ever (though the rest

Were silent).   And my days and I,
We listened, as the hours went by :
It seemed all hope could never die,

Whilst in my heart the sweet birds sang,
That therewithal the whole wood rang,
And all the thrushes with their clang

Of joyful music answered it.
Yet often through my heart would flit
A stinging fear lest it were writ

That some sad day the birds should fly
Away, and leave me there to die.
But day by day, more lovelily

The sweet notes quivered through the air ;
And day by day the singing bare,
Its wonted solace to my care.

So went the days by, one by one,
And many a year was past and done,
Until one morning, with the sun

A new sweet freshness seemed to rise,
And all things shone before our eyes,
As with the dews of Paradise.

And none the less on us took hold
An unformed hope, a joy untold :
And in our hearts, all blank and cold,

There sprang a new sweet prescience,
That was like wine of life, a sense
Of some expectant glad suspense,

A waiting, sure of its desire,
For some new gladness to transpire
And touch our pallid lips with fire.

Nor was our yearning hope belied ;
For, as the clear fresh morning died
Into the golden summer-tide

That fills the noonday, there came one
That brought into the woodlands dun
The fulfilled splendour of the sun.

Along a slope of grass she came :
And as she walked, a virgin shame
Lit up her face's snow with flame.

Full slight and small she was, and bent
Her lithe neck shyly, as she went,
In some childlike bewilderment.

Gold was the colour of her hair ;
The colour of her eyes was vair ;
The sun shone on her everywhere.

O fair she was as hawthorn-flowers !
It seemed the flush of the Spring-hours
Lay on her cheeks, and Summer-showers

Had bathed her in a sweet content,
A virginal faint ravishment
Of peace ; for with her came a scent

Of flowers plucked with a childish hand
In some forgotten Fairyland,
Where all arow the sweet years stand.

And all the creatures of the wood
Crept from their leafy solitude,
And wondering around her stood.

The fawns came to her, unafraid,
And on her hand their muzzles laid :
And fluttering birds flew down and stayed,

Singing, upon her breast and hair
Most fearlessly, and nestled there,—
Such charms of peace about her were.

Then all my weary days arose,
As doves rise from the olive-close,
When the dawn opens like a rose,

And said, " We have been sad too long :
From morning-gold to even-song,
We have bemoaned ourselves for wrong ;

" And now, the pleasant years are fled,
(Say, is our mouth the early red ?)
And our life hastens to the dead.

" And yet our yearning is unstayed.
But now the hope for which we prayed
Is found ; the comfort long-delayed

" Shines in our sight.   We will arise
And go to her ; for in her eyes
The promise of the new Spring lies.

" Lo ! this is the Deliverer,
Awearied for from year to year ;
See, the sun's sign is gold on her."

Then with a strange and sudden thrill,
A new life seemed to rise and fill
The channels of my brain, until

The old sad solitary peace
Fell off from me ; and there did cease
From round me, with a swift decrease,

The ancient agony of doubt
And yearning for the things without :
And therewithal my soul flowered out

Into a rapture of desire
Celestial; and some new sweet fire
Of hope rose in me high and higher.

For in her kind child-eyes there shone
A radiance tender as the dawn ;
And by their light my heart was drawn

To auguries of life fulfilled ;
And hope o'erleapt the line grey-hilled
That shut my days in, sad and stilled,

Into some fresh clear world beyond,
Where thought is with fulfilment crowned,
And Life to Love alone is bond.

To me she came and laid to mine
The velvet of her lips divine,
And looked into my faded eyne

With eyes that seemed to swim in gold
Of perfect passion and to hold
The Love that never shall grow cold.

And there with hers my life was made
One, as it seemed. From dell to glade,
The wild wood lifted off its shade ;

And through the aisles the frank sun leapt,
And startled out the dreams that slept,
And filled with smiles the eyes that wept.

And all my tearful days and sad
Put off their gloom, and were made glad ;
For there was that in her forbad

The sourest sorrow to abide,
Where once its place was glorified
By that clear presence sunny-eyed :

And like the wild rose after rain,
They lifted up their eyes again,
The clearer for the bygone pain,

Love-led by hers : and all their store
They gave, and taught her o'er and o'er
The secrets of their dainty lore.

So Hope and I made friends anew,
Whilst over all the morning dew
Fell down ; the clouded sky broke blue

Through tears of joy and ravishment ;
And all my lifeless life was blent
With faith and peace, what time we went,

I and my lady, hand in hand,
Where all the hours run golden sand,
In Love's enchanted Fairyland.

Ah love, how sad remembrance is
Of lips joined in the first love-kiss,
And all the wasted early bliss !

Ah, bitter sad it is to stand,
And look back to the ghostly strand,
Where our lost dreams lie hand in hand

And slumber in the grey of years !
Ah, weary sad to rain down tears
Upon their graves, until the biers

Give up to earth the much-loved dead,
And one by one, with drooping head,
Our dead hopes pass by us adread !

Each with its beauty of the Past,
Pale with long prison and aghast,
Whilst on the wind there shrills a blast

Of moaning dirges that for us
Of old were songs melodious,
Our sweet days rendered to us thus !

Ah, sadder still to live and live,
Till Death itself it seems can give
Hardly the rest for which we strive !

How long the new life lasted me,
I cannot tell : the hours did flee
Like summer winds across the sea,

Unseen, unheard ; for day was knit
To golden day, and night was lit
With such delight, I had no wit

Of Time.   The shadow of his flight
Scarce showed against the blaze of light
Wherewith love flooded day and night.

And in that new illumining
Of Hope and Faith, each precious thing,
From which the light had taken wing

In our old night of dreariment,
Put off its sadness and was blent
With our new life in ravishment.

Ah, how we loved, my days and I,
To lead her where old dreams did lie,
Buried of yore with many a sigh,—

To clear the rank grass from the tomb
And watch the dead delight out-bloom,
Lovelier than ever, from the gloom,

At one glance of her radiant eyne,
And all those desert wastes of mine,
Conscious of her, arise and shine.

So went I with her, hand in hand,
Through hall and glade of all the land ;
And everywhere at her command,

Sprang into life forgotten flowers,
Long laid asleep beneath the hours ;
And from entangling weeds, waste bowers

Of rose and woodbind blossomed out
Into new beauty, hymned about
With bird-song ; and a joyous rout

Of echoes ran from dell to dell,
Praising her presence and the spell
That like a perfume from her fell.

And at her voice the monsters fled,
That had so long, in doubt and dread,
Held my life level with the dead ;

And through the tangled forest shade,
There was, meseemed, a new way made,
In which my hope trod, unafraid,

Towards the gracious world of men,
And drank, beneath the free sun's ken,
The breath of daily life again.

And then my song-birds, if before
Their song was sweet, ah ! how much more
It rang out lovely than of yore !

For from my bosom where they lay
And measured all the weary day
With madrigal and roundelay,

I took them singing in their nest
And laid them in my lady's breast,
To sing to her their loveliest.

Thence, as we went about the ways
Of that strange wonderland, my days
And I had given our lives to raise,

Their voices filled the sun-shot air
With music such as spirits hear
Ring down the golden city's stair,

When to the new-fledged soul arise,
Bathed in the light that never dies,
The citadels of Paradise.

Ah ! dreary labour of despair
To tell again the joys that were,
The dead delights that have been fair !

When hardly can dull thought retrace,
Even in dreams, the lost love's face,
The sweetness of the vanished grace.

For lost it is to me for aye,
My dream of love born but to die,
My glimpse of Heaven so soon past by.

It seemed my bliss had worn away
Hardly a summer's space of day,
And hardly yet the full light lay

Upon my winter-wasted years,
When round my joy a mist of fears
Began to gather : in my ears

A sound of sobbing winds did sigh,
And in full sunshine clouds swept by,
Darkening the visage of the sky.

And but too surely did my soul,
Though Summer in the land was whole,
Forethink me of the coming dole :

For on my short-lived sunny tide
The shadow of old griefs would glide,
With wings of memories grey and wide

Breaking the promise of the sun :
And wraiths of ancient hopes fordone
Rose in my pathway, one by one,

Each with some mocking prophecy
Of happiness condemned to die,
As ever in the days gone by.

And voices of forgotten pain
Sang round me, with a weird refrain,
Of short-lived Summers that did wane

To dreary Autumns of despair
And winters fiercer for the fair
Lost memories of Junes that were.

And all in vain the coming fate
That in my pathway stood await
I strove to conjure from Love's gate ;

. Its omen lay upon my bliss
And stole the sweetness from Love's kiss :
I stood and looked on an abyss

That gaped to end that life of ours,
And strove in vain with lavish flowers
To stay the progress of the hours.

Even in my lady's eyes of light
I saw the presage of the night ;
And in the middle love-delight,

Bytimes across her face would flit
A shadowy sadness, past Love's wit
To slay the hidden snake in it.

At last (so prescient was my grief
Its grim fulfilment seemed relief)
The storm, that o'er my flower-time brief

So long had brooded, broke the spell
Of imminent thunder,—and I fell
Straight from Love's Heaven down to Hell.

For one sad morn, awakening,
An added sadness seemed to cling
And hover over everything ;

The sun gave but a ghost of light,
And for the funeral of the night,
The flowers seemed shrouded all in white :

And listening, full of some vague fear,
For those sweet songs that used to cheer
My saddest hours, there smote my ear

No note of birds from east to west ;
The wood was dumb : but in my breast
The ancient dirges of unrest

Began with doubled stress to tear
My heartstrings, burdened as it were
With some renewal of despair.

Then gradually into my thought
The full sad sense of all was wrought,
And starting up, alarmed, I sought

My love's hands and her lips' delight,
Aye, and her bosom's silver-white,
To heal me of my soul's affright.

Alas ! my eyes could find no trace,
Of her late presence : and her place
Was empty of my lady's grace.

How many a day my sad steps wore
The wild wood pathways and the shore,
I cannot tell : the brown sand bore

No traces of her flying feet :
But now and then the tiny beat
Of wild deer's hoofs or the retreat

Of forest creatures through the trees,
That rustled in the passing breeze,
Mimicked the sound of one that flees :

And in my heart hope sprang again,
(Ah, cruel hope !) only to wane
And leave new sharpness to my pain.

And so the weary days crept by,
Whilst in the greyness of the sky
The morning lights did rise and die,

And evening sunsets came and went
As tenderly as though they meant
To mock at my bewilderment.

But nevermore my lady's sight
Gladdened my eyes : the day and night
Went empty by of all delight.

And dumb the wild wood was and still ;
For all my birds, that wont to fill
The aisles with many a dainty trill

And gush of silver song, had fled,
Following where'er my lady led,
And left me lonely as the dead.

The colours faded from the flowers :
And in the hollow midwood bowers,
The falling footsteps of the hours

Smote on the silence like a knell,
And on my soul the shadow fell
And lay there, irrevocable.

For Love, the sun of life, had set,
And nevermore should morning let
The sunshine for me through the net

That coming death had drawn about
My weary head.   Despair and doubt
Reigned in me, since Love's light was out.

Will she return, my lady?   Nay :
Love's feet, that once have learned to stray,
Turn never to the olden way.

Ah heart of mine, where lingers she?
By what live stream or saddened sea?
What wild-flowered swath of sungilt lea

Do her feet press, and are her days
Sweet with new stress of love and praise,
Or sad with echoes of old lays?

Me-knoweth not : but this I know,
My wan face haunts her in the glow
Of sunset, and my sad eyes grow

Athwart the darkness on her sight,
When in the middle hush of night
She sees the shadow grow moon-white.

And in the pauses of a kiss,
There smite her, like a serpent's hiss
From out piled flowers, the memories

Of all our passion of the past :
And then her face grows white and ghast,
And all her summer is o'ercast

With shadows of the dead delight :
A little while, in her despite,
The old love claims again its right ;

Her soul is one again with mine ;
And gladly would she then resign
Her heedless life of summer-shine,

To seek once more the silent nest,
Wherein my life is laid, and rest
Her weary head upon my breast.

But ah ! the way is all o'ergrown
With underwoods, and many a stone
Blocks up the pathway, shadow-strown ;

And never may she win to me,
Nor I to her : Eternity
Is spread betwixt us like a sea.

For Love, that pardoneth not, hath ta'en
Back to himself the golden chain
That bound our lives ; and ne'er again,

Nor in this life of hours and days,
Nor in that hidden world that stays
For us beyond the grave-grown ways,

Our hands shall join, our lips shall meet ;
Never again with aught of sweet
Shall our twinned hearts together beat.

But through the mists of life and death,
The sorrow that remembereth
Shall haunt her, and the very breath

Of heaven be bitter to her spright,
(Grown sadder for its clearer sight)
For memories laden with despite

Of that lost love so lightly seen,
So lightly left, that might have been
The fairest flower of heaven's sheen.

BALLAD OF PAST DELIGHT.

WHERE are the dreams of the days gone by,
  The hopes of honour, the glancing play
Of fire-new fancies that filled our sky,
    The songs we sang in the middle May,
    Carol and ballad and roundelay?
Where are the garlands our young hands twined?
    Life's but a memory, well-a-way!
All else flits past on the wings of the wind.

Where are the ladies fair and high—
    Marie and Alice and Maud and May
And merry Madge with the laughing eye—
    And all the gallants of yesterday
    That held us merry—ah where are they?
Under the mould we must look to find
    Some; and the others are worn and grey.
All else flits past on the wings of the wind.

I know of nothing that lasts, not I,
   Save a heart that is true to its love alway—
A love that is won with tear and sigh
   And never changes or fades away,
   In a breast that is oftener sad than gay ;
A tender look and a constant mind—
   These are the only things that stay.
All else flits past on the wings of the wind.

ENVOI.

Prince, I counsel you, never say
   Alack for the years that are left behind !
Look you keep love when your dreams decay ;
   All else flits past on the wings of the wind.

RONDEAU.

ONE of these days, my lady whispereth,
　　A day made beautiful with Summer's breath,
Our feet shall cease from these divided ways,
Our lives shall leave the distance and the haze
And flower together in a mingling wreath.
No pain shall part us then, no grief amaze,
No doubt dissolve the glory of our gaze;
Earth shall be heaven for us twain, she saith,
　　　　One of these days.

　　Ah love, my love ! Athwart how many Mays
The old hope lures us with its long delays !
How many winters waste our fainting faith !
I wonder, will it come this side of death,
With any of the old sun in its rays,
　　　　One of these days ?

SAD SUMMER.

A H Summer, lady of the flowered lands,
       When shall thy lovely looks bring back to me
   —To me who strain into the grey sad sea
Of dreams unsatisfied, and with stretched hands
Implore the stern sky and the changeless sands
       For some faint sign of that which was to be
       So perfect and so fair a life to see —
The time of songs and season of flower-bands ?

At least, for guerdon of full many a lay
       In praise of thee and of thy youngling Spring,
       What time my lips were yet attuned to sing,
Let not thy roses redden in my way
Too flauntingly, nor all thy golden day
       Insult my silence with too glad a ring.

BALLAD OF LOVE'S DESPITE.

I.

IN my young time, full many a lady bright
   I wooed, and recked but little how I sped.
Was one unkind, it caused me small despite ;
    With careless heart a light " Farewell " I said,
    And wooed another maiden in her stead.
Thus fared I joyously and thought no wrong
To mock at lovers in a jesting song,
    And heeded not if one to me did say,
" Beware ! Love's bliss endureth not for long ;
    Love's sadness lasts for ever and a day !"

II.

I made a mock of Love and his delight,
   Called it a fever of fond fancies bred,
And women toys, too idle and too slight
   To be remembered, when desire was dead.
   Alack ! the sword hung o'er me by a thread ;
I too must kneel among the love-lorn throng
And prove how high Love's power is and how
   strong.
   For lo ! I loved a maiden bright and gay
And learnt, alas ! though Love be little long,
   Love's sadness lasts for ever and a day !

III.

True, she loved me in turn ; and life was light
   For many a day, whilst in her eyes I read
The sweet confession of Love's rosy might :
   But soon, alas ! her flitting fancy fled
   And settled lightly on another's head.
Ah, who so hapless then as I ! Among
The woods I wandered, smarting 'neath the thong
   Of his fell scourge, and wailing out alway
The old refrain, " Love's bliss is little long ;
   Love's sadness lasts for ever and a day !"

ENVOI.

Prince, in delight that walk'st the world along,

Chiefest of those that unto Love belong !

　　Take heed unto the burden of my lay

And know, Love's pleasance is but little long ;

　　Love's sadness lasts for ever and a day.

RONDEL.

THE year has cast its wede away
  Of rain, of tempest and of cold,
  And put on broidery of gold
Of sunbeams bright and clear and gay.
There is no bird or beast to-day
  But sings and shouts in field and fold,
" The year has cast its wede away
  Of rain, of tempest and of cold.'

The silver fret-work of the May
  Is over brook and spring enscrolled,
  A blazon lovely to behold.
Each thing has put on new array :
The year has cast its wede away
  Of rain, of tempest and of cold.

From Charles d'Orléans.

THE LAST OF THE GODS.

THE world is worn with many weary years ;
  The day is dim for long desire of death :
Life languishes amid its burning breath
Of nights and days, of barren hopes and fears,
Of joys that sing in vain to listless ears.
  For Love and Spring are dead for lack of faith ;
  And in the bird-songs goes a voice that saith,
" Who shall absolve us of this life of tears ?"
Ah, who indeed ? Who shall avail to save
  Our souls that wither on the wrecks of life ?
Is any strong among the Gods men crave
Enough to take again the gifts He gave,
  To draw death like a dream upon our strife,
And soothe the sick world to its grateful grave ?

II.

Ah, who shall hope, when God Himself implores,
  With piteous hands, the unremorseful sleep,—
  When Gods and men, from one abysmal deep
Of loveless life, lift hands toward the shores
Of the unnearing rest—through Time, that roars
  With wave on wave of years to come—and weep
  In undistinguished anguish, as they keep
Life's hopeless vigil at Death's stirless doors !
Lo ! of all Gods that men have knelt unto,—
  Of all the dread Immortals fierce and fair,
That men have painted on the vault of blue,—
  There is but one remains, of all that were.
Death hath put on their crowns ; and to him sue
  Mortals and Gods in parity of prayer.

RONDEAU.

LIFE lapses by for you and me,
   Our sweet days pass us by and flee,
And evermore Death draws us nigh :
The blue fades fast out of our sky,
The ripple ceases from our sea.
What would we not give, you and I,
The early sweet of life to buy !
Alas ! sweetheart, that cannot we ;
         Life lapses by.

   But though our young years buried lie,
Shall love with Spring and Summer die ?
What if the roses faded be !
We in each other's eyes will see
New Springs, nor question how or why
         Life lapses by.

GHAZEL.

LADY of beauty, that dost take all hearts with
    thy disdain
And slay'st with stress of love the souls that sigh for
    thee in vain,
If thou recall me not to mind beyond our parting
    day,   \
God knows the thought of thee with me for ever shall
    remain.
Thou smitest me with cruel words, that yet are sweet
    to me ;
Wilt thou one day vouchsafe to me thy sweetest sight
    again ?
I had not thought the ways of Love were languish-
    ment and woe
And stress of soul, before, alas ! to love thee I was
    fain.

Even my foes have ruth on me and pity my distress ;

But thou, O heart of steel, wilt ne'er have mercy on
my pain !

By God, although I die, I'll ne'er be comforted for
thee !

Though Love itself should fail, my love shall never
pass or wane !

From the Arabic.

SALVESTRA.

13

Girolamo ama la Salvestra : va, costretto da
prieghi della madre, a Parigi : torna e truovala
maritata : entrale di nascosto in casa, e muorle
allato ; e, portato in una chiesa, muore la Salvestra
allato a lui.

Boccaccio—Il Decamerone, Giorn. iv. 8.

\

SALVESTRA.

A II, *Love, thou art but as a Summer's guest,*
  That long before the Winter fleest away
And in some warmer haven harbourest,
  Nipt by the hard swift life of our To-day !
  Our love is scant and flowerless as our May,
And will not lightly let its pinions soil
Their rainbow plumes in our unblissful toil.

  Time was, fair God, when thou heldst fuller sway,
And all folk were thy thralls in gentilesse :
  Time was when men were simpler than to-day,
And life was not one fierce and loveless stress
Of unrelenting labour in the press
  Of joyless souls, when men had time to rest
  And toy with grace and beauty, unreprest.

Full sweet, ah! hopeless sweet, to us it seems—
    Fast bounden in a mesh of strife and care—
That time of graceful ease and builded dreams,
    Seen in a glamour through the misted air ;
    Through which sweet strains of song the breezes bear.
And scents of flowers that then were full and blythe,
But now are mown away by Time's swift scythe.

    And yet it was no golden age, that time :
Not unalloyed with pain and doubt and strife :
    But through all ventures ran the gold of rhyme,
And Love was high and was the Lord of Life.
From Venice-turrets unto Algarsife,
    All held fair deeds and lovely worshipful,
    And all were scholars in Love's gracious school.

Then men did honour Love with heart and soul,
    Setting their lives upon his smile or frown ;
For in their hearts his altar-flame was whole
    And burnt unchanged until Life's sun went down.
    Love was the flower of life and honour's crown,
Wherewith men perfumed all the weary years
And purged the air from mean and sordid fears.

Then men, as they for very Love could live,
So for the death of very Love could die,
    Holding it shame to let the rank flesh give
.Commandment to the swift soul's fantasy ;
And for the love of him they held so high,
    Did woo and win, with fair and potent faith,
    The soft embraces of his brother Death.

A sad sweet tale is hovering in my thought,
    A tale of perfect love in death fulfilled,
From out the waves of sweeping Time upbrought
    By that enchanter of the past, who filled
    The ears of men with music sweet and wild,
When in the world he breathed strange scents upon
That sheaf of flowers men call Decameron.

A tale in dreams, heard betwixt wake and sleep,
Under the tremulous shadow of the planes :
    Attuned to rhythmic cadence by the sweep
Of murmurous rillets through the scented lanes
Of rose and jasmine—sweep of wings and strains
    Of happy linnets piping to the rose—
    And chirp of crickets in the olive-close.

O Master, of whose speech in that green time,
   Heard under shredded laurels and faint flowers,
I took the echo for my painful rhyme,
   To warm it in this cold hard time of ours,
   Whose plagues no wall of rose or lys outbowers—
Let not thy laureat brow be rough with frown,
If I unleave thy honeysuckle crown

   With my interpreting.   Sweet is the will,
And all fair-meaning as a day in June,
   The faded accords of thy song to fill
And echo back that magical sweet tune
Thou sangest in the garden's golden noon,
   With youths and maidens lying, myrtle-crowned,
   Upon the flower-glad carpet of the ground.

But ah ! the air is faint with weariness
   Of toil, and love has grown a doubtful dream,
That now no longer, type of holiness,
   Regilds the shapes of faded things that seem
   And are not in our world !   The sad ghosts stream
Towards the darkness ; and my sense can seize
No touch of reverent peace or graceful ease,

No waft of tender fancy in the sky,
No Phœbus standing, dawn-red, on the hill—
And must e'en feed itself on memory,
And with those strains of old its yearning fill,
Whose echo at my heart-strings lingers still—
Unable to revive the ancient flame,
Sadly some pale ghost of its brightness frame.

Fair flowery city, peerless in the world,
    Germ-garden of the golden blooms of Art,
But seldom have thy myrtle-groves impearled
    So fair a creature in their flowerful heart
    As young Salvestra.   Could my song impart
Her manifold perfections, well I deem
My verse should glow with glories of a dream.

So fair she was, there is no rose so fair
    That in the noon drinks colour from the sun :
No flower could match the hyacinths of her hair,
    Fresh from the webs of night and morning spun :
    Her eyes were lakes, whereon, when day is done.
The slow night comes with halt and timorous pace,
And dim dreams fill the enchanted interspace.

There was the house of dreams; and on her brow—
    Clear as the marge of that cool well where Pan
Was wont to play with Pitys—broad and low
    With trellised ringlets—ended and began
    All glamours that can charm the heart of man :
There was the crystal dwelling of the Loves,
And there bright Venus fed her golden doves.

What hues can paint her mouth, what words express
    The ivory shaft of her most perfect throat ?
And what her bosom's rounded perfectness ?
    That with the heaving breath did swell and float,
    As if its snows had lately learnt by rote
The rapturous carol of some woodland bird,
And to the cadence ever mutely stirrèd.

The very sun did gently look on her
    And only kissed, not burnt, her crystal brows :
Among her locks the flower-breathed winds did stir
    And filled them with the perfumes of the rose
    And scents of foreign sweets that no man knows
But haply ravished from those plains of spice
That lengthen out the glades of Paradise.

So fair she was, her sight had virtue in 't :
  The vision of her face was used to stir
Strange deeps of love.   Full many a heart of flint
  Was softened, when men's eyes did look on her
  Like violets in the morning of the year,
There was a perfume went from her that drew
Men's careworn souls to tender thoughts and true.

If all things loved her, even the fierce sun,
  And breezes for her wooing came from far,
How should Girolamo's young bosom shun
  The keen sweet shaft of Love's unpardoning star,
  Wherewith so many hearts enwounded are?
Or how play traitor to the general fate,
He, whom the heavens had surely made for mate

Of that unparagoned brightness?   If on earth
  The gods had guerdoned and appointed one
To be conjoined with her in house of birth,
  Girolamo was sure that Fortune's son.
  His life, with hers in equal hour begun,
Had from the same breast drawn its aliment,
And all the currents of their youth were blent

Within a common channel.   Childhood was
   Dual for them with doubled love and pain ;
And with unseparate course the years did pass
   For them along the primrose-tufted plain
   Of early youth ; till, when the rise and wane
Of the recurrent Springs began to tend
Towards that spot where times of childhood end,

Where laughing girl puts on grave womanhood
   And youth is sudden man, the innocent ties,
That had so long entwined the two, renewed
   Their power.   As thought grew in Salvestra's eyes,
   The ancient childish amity did rise
In his young breast the olden banks above,
And swelled into a deep and passionate love.

If she was dark as Night, and vague and rare
   As star-bright evening thick with netted lights,
He was as frank and bright and golden-fair
   As a May morn, when on the sapphire heights
   Of heaven the young day comes with all delights
And tender glories of the dewy dawn,
And wild flowers wake on every woodland lawn.

It seemed the sun shone always on his brow,
    Among his locks' full-clustered tender gold,
Whose every shadow with rich light did glow;
    And his true eyes were cast in passion's mould,
    So fair a deep of love, all aureoled
With hope, did lurk within their amethyst,
Whose lids Diana might have stooped and kiss'd.

There looked from out his face so clear a spring
    Of love and youth, so pure and undefiled
By care or baseness, that no birds that sing
    Among the trellis—when the boughs are piled
    With blossom and the sweet lush vines run wild
With early clusters—cared to hide from him,
If to the carol of their morning hymn

He crept to listen through the flush of flowers;
    No fawn but laid the velvet of its mouth
Upon his beckoning hand: the fear that sours
    All creatures at man's aspect ('spite the drouth
    Of love that habits all the sunny South)
Fled from him, as the plague flies from the breath
Of some sweet fragrance, enemy to Death.

There was in him a candid fearlessness
  And frank delight of love, that drew men back,
Regarding him, from out the cheerlessness
  Of modern life, along the dim years' track
  To the old age, when hate nor fear nor rack
Of rueful discord held the enchanted air,
But all were loving, kind and debonair;

When love was not a virtue, but a sense,
  A natural impulse of untainted souls,
That had no thought of praise or recompense
  For what was but an instinct—and the goals,
  Towards which our life's sore-troubled current rolls,
Had not yet darkened all the innocent air
With lurid lights of greed and lust and care.

To him to love was natural as life :
  He drew in passion with his daily breath ;
Affection was his food, and hate and strife
  To him the very atmosphere of death :
  His soul was one of those to which the faith
In love and friendship is a part of being,
And—that withdrawn—there is for them no fleeing

From anguish and the death-stroke of despair :
    Once hurt, they have but strength enough to die,
Since in life's desert there is nothing fair
    For them, when love has lost its potency
    And the first dream has vanished from the sky.
And so he loved as (men do say) of old
The first folk loved, within the age of gold.

There was no like respondence of delight
    In fair Salvestra ; for her weaker mood
Sufficed not for the all-subduing might
    Of love that raged in his more ardent blood ;
    Her earthlier nature from that angels' food
Of perfect passion ever failed and shrank.
She knew not Love, though at her eyes he drank,

Though in her mouth his flowers were fresh and red,
    His magic in each tangle of her hair
Was hidden ; all was cold as are the dead,
    And no one note of ecstasy was there,
    To stir to splendour the unthrobbing air.
No glamours of the tender haze of love
Lay ever those clear orbs of hers above,

Such as are sweeter to a lover's gaze
    Than brightest radiance of untroubled bliss—
No touch of tender sadness, such as lays
    Soft lips to lips with such a rapturous kiss.
    In her most glorious face, the soul did miss
The informing ardour of some subtle charm,
Whose absence chilled the Summer sweet and warm

That there bloomed ever : and the missing note
    Left to the wish, in every harmony
Of loveliness that round her face did float,
    A formless longing, as of some sweet sky,
    In whose moon-flooded purple canopy
Of silver star-work set in amethyst,
The very star of evening should be miss'd.

They were alike unequal in estate.
    His father was a merchant of renown,
That had held highest office in the state ;
    For whom a name of honour, handed down
    Through many an ancestor, had slowly grown
And ripened to great increase of repute :
In him the tree had born its fairest fruit

Of worship.   He had of his native town
  Been three times prior : wealth and dignities
Had bound his temples with a various crown
    Of splendid memories.   His argosies
    Had swept for treasure all the Indian seas,
Heaping his hands with gorgeous pearl and gold
And ingots cast in many an Orient mould.

So for Girolamo there was prepared
    A goodly heritage, and his ripening age
Might to all heights of eminence have dared
    To look for honour and all noble rage
    For dignities have counted to assuage,
Being by birth set in that charmed ring,
Wherein the flowers of honour use to spring.

His foster-sister was that fairest one :
    She was the daughter of a clothworker,
Unto whose wife his little weakling son,
    Born well-nigh in an equal hour with her,
    Girolamo's own sire did, many a year,
Commit for fosterance ; and so the twain
Together knew life's earliest joy and pain.

Surely some power had breathed strange spells on
    them,
  To weave their fortunes in a mingled skein ;
Some flower of Fate had blossomed on its stem
    A double calyx, in some sweet domain
    Of herbs and charms where (as old fables feign)
Fair wives do sit and weave with knitted flowers
The changeful fortunes of this life of ours ;

With knitted wreaths, not woven all of rose
    Or lavish jasmine in the gold of June,
Or delicate sweetness of the flower that blows
    In April, when the harsh winds breathe in tune
    To Spring's fresh music and the ways are strewn
With violets. Rosemary is there and rue
And sad-eyed scabious with the petals blue.

There cypress grows for garlands funeral ;
    And there the dim and tearful lilies blow ;
Sad hemlock for dead lovers' coronal,
    And nightshade, bitter at the heart for woe.
    There not alone the lark and linnet throw
Spring's wealth of music on the enamoured air,
And throstles sing that Summer is most fair ;

14—2

But there full oft the widowed nightingale
   Lengthens her holy sadness into song ;
And many a night-bird fills the air with wail :
   Dead love sings there with cadence sad and long,
   And there the dread sweet tunes are clear and strong,
That in the hearts of weary folk are dumb ;
Since sorrow is too fair to have outcome

In its most perfect strain from mortal throat,
   Or dare with its most holy notes and pure
The gross encounter of this world of rote,
   Where men know not the sweets its pains procure.
   So in this garden only doth endure
Divinity of sadness, 'mid the throng
Of joyful sounds a holy intersong.

Surely, the nymphs that wove the earthly fate
   Of these two lovers,—whilst their white hands played
With amaranths and violets and the state
   Of roses for the crown of youth and maid,—
   Had heard these singing that the rose must fade,
Nesh violets wither from their fragrant bloom
Nor amaranths of love evade death's doom ;

And sighing, laid a rose or two aside
   And chosen herbs of sadness and of woe,
White wind-flowers and pale pansies, dreamy-eyed,
   And evergreens of cypress, that do blow
   When all green else has withered from the snow,—
Mindful that love is fed with Summer's breath,
But sorrow dies not, though the air be death.

\

The star of lovers, that upon the birth
   Of these two lovelings shed its saddest rays,
Had but thenceforward glimmered on the earth
   A little span of nights and equal days,
   When from his walking in the pleasant ways
Of life his father ceased, and did commit
Unto his widow's care, in all things fit

For his son's heritage to govern him.
   And she, a noble lady, fair and high,
Queenlike in goodly port and graceful limb,
    But hard and stern withal, did her apply
    Unto the matter well and faithfully,
Ordering his state and household passing well,
In all the things where need to her befell.

So for Girolamo the first years went
   Peacefully by in pleasance and delight,
And all his years of youth he was content
    To dwell with her his mother; nor despite
    The heat of youthful blood, did aught invite
His peaceful thought to seek to be set free
From her control or larger liberty.

For such a perfect passion filled his heart,
   So strong and therewithal so innocent,
That in his hope no thing could have a part,
    Wherewith Salvestra's presence was unblent;
    And all his thought on her was so intent,
It seemed his youth should never pass away,
Whilst in her eyes love met him day by day.

He sought no fellowship with anyone,
   Bearing no share in chase or revelry;
But in his love's companionship alone
   He lived, disdaining all delights that she
   Must leave unshared, and careful but to be
Beloved of her : for him, she being kind,
No other thing could touch his constant mind.

For him, the treasure of her love contained
   And did annul with its most perfect light
All things for which he saw men sought and
      strained.
   There was to him no other ear-delight
   Than her sweet speech, no other charm of sight
Than her fair presence, and (she being gone)
No bliss save dreams of her from dusk to dawn.

His life to her was wholly consecrate ;
   She had no hope in which he did not share ;
She was for either sorry or elate ;
   So twinned he was to her in joy and care,
   It seemed as if some charm upon him were,
Whereby his soul its stature had forgone,
And for pure love her weakness had put on.

How should a lover of such perfect fire
   As this fair youngling, in the blush and heat
Of the first passion, find aught to desire
   In her that lets herself be loved? So sweet
   It was to love, he could no more entreat
Than she would give him look for look and kiss
For longing kiss, and from the deep abyss

Of his unfailing passion could supply
   Unconsciously the warmth that lacked in her,
Holding her coldness in such constancy
   And ceaseless ardentness of love, the stir
   Of the celestial flame that folded her,
Kissing her marble with ethereal fire,
Some semblance raised of its own pure desire.

And at her feet, in that unsullied time,
   The golden harvest of his young life's Spring
He laid, outpouring all the lavish prime
   Of his first hope, the bright ingathering
   Of that clear time of youth, when every thing
Blossoms to beauty with the radiant hours
And all the thoughts are lovely unknown flowers.

He made his love for her one long sweet song
   Of various cadence, filling every break
Of gradual days with many a glittering throng
    Of flower-new fancies, till, as some grey brake
    From Spring's soft hands its robe of blooms doth
       take,
Her lesser life caught blossom at his smile
And seemed all glorified with love awhile.

So for a few sweet years their lives were blent
   In mingled ways of love and innocence,
And no fear came to mar the sweet content
    Of that untroubled season ; but their sense
    Slept in a linked enchantment, folded dense
And sweet as Summer-woods, that stand screen-wise
Betwixt the world and some clear Paradise

Ah lovely time of love and purity !
   April before the summer heats draw nigher !
What thing on earth is pleasant like to thee,
    Whilst yet the veils lie folded round the fire
    Of the insatiate conquering Desire,
When all things tremble with the dews of Spring
And love is mystery and wondering ?

Ah ! frail as sweet thy tender blossoms are !
   Shortlived as primroses that blow in Spring
And die whilst yet the Summer shines afar
   Nor May has set the swallows on the wing.
   Thy strain is as the birds' descant that sing
In haunted woods a dreamy song and clear
And cease, if any stay his steps to hear.

For years, none knew the bondage of delight
   That bound these lovers (nor themselves as yet
Perchance had learnt to name their ties aright ;)
   But unobserved of any eye they met
   And took their ease of kiss and amorette ;
Till, at the last, chance broke the happy spell
Of secrecy ; and on this wise it fell

The palace, where for many years bygone
   His ancestors had dwelt, a little space
Without the city's ramparts stood withdrawn,
   Fronting the silver river with the grace
   Of its tall turrets, wreathed on every face
With flowers and shrubs, through which the white
      house shone,
Like some dream-stead the sunset lies upon.

Hard by the house a little wood there was,
  Towards which the garden sloped its slow descent
Adown long sunny banks of smoothen grass,
  With chalices of Summer thick besprent ;
  And through the sward a silver brooklet went
And made sweet music to the amorous breeze,
Until it wound among the shadowing trees.

Full of bird-song and scent of forest-flowers
  The coppice was, and very sweet and cool
In the hot noontide were its trellised bowers,
  Set by the glass of some dream-haunted pool,
  Whereon the sleepy sweetness of the lull
Of silence brooded ; and its every glen
Was set with purple of the cyclamen

Or starred with white of amaryllis blooms,
  Pale flower-dreams of the virginal green sward,
That made faint sweetness in the emerald glooms :
  And through the stillness ever rose and soared
  The song of some up-mounting lark, that poured
The gold of his delight for rose-hung June
Into the channel of a perfect tune.

Here did these lovers often use to walk,
  Calling the flowers to witness of their love,
Mocking, in sport, with sweet and murmurous talk,
  The tender cooing of the amorous dove,
  That filled the arches of the boughs above
And echoed through the cloisters,—sat anon
Upon some lilied bank, and there did con,

In rapturous silence, every lovely look,
  Each blush of eloquent cheek and glow of eyes,
Reading sweet stories in that lover's book
  Of joining faces, with soft wind of sighs
  To fan their joyance,—as a breeze that dies,
Bending two neighbour roses till they meet,—
And now all sunned with laughters low and sweet.

It chanced, one Summer, as these lovers went
  For joyance in the pleasant woodland ways,—
Rejoicing in the tender thymy scent
  And in the sweet attemperance of the blaze
  Of noon that reigned within the forest maze,—
The Countess walked, for ease of the fierce heat,
In that fair garden, where the lawns were sweet

With lavish fall of rose-leaves ; and anon
  The cool sweet promise of the wood did woo
Her feet to enter where the sunlight shone
  Athwart thick leafage and the sky showed blue
  'Twixt rifted boughs; and walking thus, she knew
The sound of voices mingled in converse
Murmurous and sweet, as birds that did rehearse

Some new sweet descant for the ear of night:
  And listening closelier, as the voices drew
The nearer, she was ware that Love's delight
  Was theme of that soft speaking, and she knew
  The silver speech of kisses, that ensue
The vows of love, as music follows on
With strain on strain, in some sweet antiphon ;

And curious to know what folk these were,
  That walked in woods for love and solacement,
Under the shadow of the boughs drew near
  Beside the shaded path, where, all intent
  Each upon each, hand-linked these lovers went :
So low they spoke, she could not catch their words
Aright, for clatter of the clamouring birds

And gurgle of the stream betwixt the trees.
　　But in the middle way the sun had found
A place of branches rifted by the breeze,
　　And stealing through the opening to the ground,
　　Had thrown a pool of golden light around ;
And as the twain passed where the sunlight shone,
She recognised Salvestra and her son.

Then much despite gat hold upon her soul,
　　And sorely she was troubled in her mind ;
For shame it seemed to her and bitter dole
　　That thus a low-born maiden had entwined
　　Her son with arts ; and sore she sought to find
Some means whereby he should be won to break
The chains he wore for sweet Salvestra's sake.

Crouched in the shadow of the thickset leaves,
　　She waited, while the twain passed on their way
Out of the wood ; and where the forest-eaves
　　Bent o'er the highway, there she saw them lay
　　Lips unto lips, as 'twere the last that day :
And then they parted, she towards the town
Wending, with hasting feet and girded gown.

But he a little stood, with longing eyes
   Following her form along the highway's white,
Until,—when all the power in Love that lies
   Availed not to retain her in his sight,—
   Sighing as one that lapses from delight,
He pushed the gate that opened from the street,
And wandered up the garden with slow feet.

And wandering thus, he came to where the fount
   Smote the blue air with one thin silver spire,
And in like gracious fashion did dismount
   Into the jewelled pool, that lay afire
   With golden carp,—and rising again higher,
Did seem to image some fair perfect love,
That, lowlier stooping, soars the more above.

And there beside the tinkle of the stream
   Himself he laid upon the rose-strewn grass,
And in the sweet ensuing of his dream
   Of bliss, saw not his mother that did pass
   Swiftly by him, with mien and look, alas !
That of a truth forebode despite and ill
To that fair love that all his thoughts did fill.

Ah, Love! Ah, fair god Love! it wearieth me
To think how many work to do thee ill,—
How many in this grey sad world there be
That strive alway thy gracious power to kill
And hinder those that work thy gentle will!
Forsooth, it is great wonder that away
From earth thou hast not fled this many a day.

For of a truth, fair God, my heart is sad
For these two lovers and the coming blight
That those that hate thy gentle spells and glad
Have conjured up to slay their heart's delight;
And much it irks me that the goodly light
Of such a sweet Spring-day should change and fade,
For men's despite, to death's unfriendly shade.

And yet take heart, God of the soul's delight!
No hate shall slay thy tender empery:
The day is not more sure of the sun's light
Nor Spring of flowers, than that there aye shall be
Maidens and youths to offer prayers to thee,—
Ay, sure as death,—and singers, too, to sing
In every age of Love's fair triumphing.

So in all lovers' names and in the name
    Of all true men that set their hearts to song,
I lay a life-long curse on those that frame
    Sad wiles and false to poison Love with wrong
    And wear out passion with the anguish long
Of parting,—ay, grey life I invoke for them
And death unsanctified by requiem

Of choiring linnets. Never flower of Spring
    Shall blossom in their lives, nor fruit of peace
Ripen their summer long to harvesting;
    But with the years their sadness shall increase
    And shadow them : and when dull life shall cease,
Their heads shall lie unmemoried in the gloom,
Nor lovers wander by their flowerless tomb.

But that fair haughty lady, being come
　　Into the house, began to cast about
Within herself to bring to pass the doom
　　　　Of parting for these lovers : without doubt
　　　　It seemed to her, that if she opened out
Her mind to him, he could not choose but bow
' Unto her will, as always until now.

But first, intent upon a milder way,
　　She sought Girolamo, and so began
To work towards her wish with words that lay
　　　　Like foam upon the waves and overran
　　　　Her purpose, saying that well-nigh a man
He now was grown, and now the need was great
That he should presently to man's estate

Advance himself in things of daily use
　　And knowledge of the ways and works of men,
To end that he might fit himself to choose
　　　　Some station in the world, coming to ken
　　　　All things wrought out with sword and speech and
　　　　　　pen,
And all the stir of folk, that day by day
Beat up the wave of life to foam and spray.

And meet it seemed (to him she did pursue)
   That for the better ripening of his youth
In all things liberal and knowledge due,
   He should leave idling in that sunny South,—
   That treacherous mother with the red bane-mouth,–
And for awhile in lands of colder air
Renew his thought and learn new senses there.

But he took little heed of her discourse,
   Hearing her speech but as a devious dream,
That through the channels of a sleep doth course,
   With trains of doubtful words, that do but seem
   And leave no memory by the morning's beam ;
And all the while he answered not or made
Some mutter of reply, that nothing weighed.

Till, for her useless wiles, the pent-up spite
   Began to break the chains of prudentness,
And with harsh words unto the hapless wight
   She did pour forth her heart's full bitterness
   Against Salvestra and her rage no less
Against himself, upbraiding him full sore
For those fond foolish fetters that he wore.

And ended by commandment laid on him
   That he should do her bidding in this wise,
And for awhile,—until the thought grew dim
   Of that his folly,—under foreign skies
   Avoid the witchcraft of Salvestra's eyes ;
So haply, being come to man's estate,
He should have wit to choose a worthier mate.

And adding many a false and feignèd tale,
   She did oppress his sad and aching ears,
Until at last with lies she did prevail
   Upon her son to yield his will to hers
   And lose his lady's sight for two long years,
Wherein she hoped Salvestra should be wed,
Or else the love of her in him be dead.

Therewith Girolamo, enforced by guile,
   Took leave of that fair Florence and the sight
Of his Salvestra,—and full many a mile
   Journeying by land and sea, unto that bright
   And goodly city came, that Paris hight,
Wherein all loveliest ladies use to dwell,
And many a fair lord of whom men tell.

For, of a truth, in that fair country France
   Has ever been the home of love and song :
There knights have done fair deeds with sword and
      lance ;
   And if by hazard any suffer wrong,
   I' faith therein he shall not suffer long,
Nor any lady lack to be redrest,
Whilst any lord of France have spear in rest.

And verily, if they be brave and fair,—
   The knights and damozels that dwell therein,—
The land is beautiful beyond compare
   And worthy of its children : therewithin
   The earth is thick with lilies, and the din
Of nightingales and every sweet-voiced bird
All night among its rose-gardens is heard.

And of that goodly land, the pearl of flowers,
   The queen-rose of the garland Paris is,
Paris white-walled, that from its fragrant bowers
   Rises tall-steepled, full of pleasaunces
   And gardens sweet with jasmine and with lys,
And palaces that glitter in the air,
Less fair alone than ladies dwelling there.

Paris, whose life is like a dream-delight
   Of splendid memories, where the very walls,
Glowing with old-world splendours, charm the sight
    With tales of hero-life ; and trumpet-calls
    Re-echo from the golden-fretted halls,
Telling how women loved and men were strong,
And poets set their lives in golden song.

Two dragging years, two full-told weary years
   In that fair town Girolamo did dwell
Unwillingly,—for all his mind with fears
    Was racked, and on his thought the cruel spell
    Of some vague misery lay, and made a hell
Of every thing and every pleasant spot,
Where the fair face of her he loved was not.

Nor was there any damozel so fair
   Of all the lovely ladies that he saw
Walk beautiful about the gardens there,
    Or ride a-hawking in green field and shaw,
    That could anew subdue him to Love's law :
He counted all their lovely looks for nought,
For his love's face was ever in his thought.

And so, when those two weary years were past.
  Wherein he had been exiled from delight,
And he was free to turn his feet at last
    To Florence, well I wot his heart was light
    To think he should regain Salvestra's sight;
And not a thought of sorrow held his mind,
For all the pleasant things he left behind.

But with a heart inflamed with long desire
    And love that on itself so long had fed,
That it had taken for its food of fire
    All other thoughts, across the sea he sped
    And came to Florence, wearying to tread
The earth that bore Salvestra, and to press
Once more within his arms her loveliness.

Alas! he thought not what a hapless thing
    Is absence, and how easily far love
Is apt to fall off from remembering.
    Knowing there was no creature fair enough
    Nor any chance that could prevail above
The fortress of his heart, how should he fear
Less constancy in her he held so dear?

So, when he knew, as very soon he knew,
  (Ah me, ill hap hath no relenting wing !)
That she, by whom alone the sky was blue
  And the day sweet to him,—dishonouring
  Her plighted faith to him,—was wed with ring,—
The fulness of his misery smote him not
At first.   As one that in the heart is shot

So suddenly that at the first he seems
  Untouched by wound, yet presently he falls
Stone-dead,—or like a man that walks in dreams
  And sees each thing that unto him befalls
  As others' fortune,—through the palace-halls
He went, all dazed, among old memories,
As one that looks and knows not what he sees.

And at his heart some vague disease did gnaw,
  Sapping the springs of life, so that he cared
For nought, nor took delight in aught he saw
  Or heard ; but like a soul in doom he fared
  Aimlessly here and there, and no man dared
To stay his feet or strive to comfort him ;
For all his gentle visage pale and grim

Was grown; and if one spoke to him, he gazed
  A moment in his face with witless eyes,
But answered not, and left him all amazed.
  Even when his mother pressed him,—weary-wise
  He broke from her, filling the air with sighs :
And for the indulgence of his lonely mood,
He did betake himself into the wood.

And there, at last, the sweet familiar dells
  And woodways, where he wont to walk of old
With his Salvestra,—and the rewrought spells
  Of bird's descant and flowers and summer-gold,
  Wherewith his happy memories were enscrolled
(That now, alas ! were poison), broke his trance
And made him ware of all his heavy chance.

And when at length the full and fatal sense
  Of all his misery possessed his brain,
The anguish of wanhope was so intense,
  That his weak body failed him for the pain :
  Well-nigh it wrought to break the enfeebled chain
Of life ; and in a fever, many a day,
Nigh unto death unconsciously he lay.

But yet the strength of his supreme desire
   Once more to look upon his lady's face,
Mightier than death, prevailed against the fire
   Of that fell sickness : with a halting pace,
   Sad life came back to its accustomed place,
And from his bed he rose, a weary man,
Wasted with fever, pale and weak and wan.

And for the staying of his longing pain,
   Bethought him first where he might chance to meet
Salvestra's eyes and hear her voice again :
   For he could not believe, the memories sweet
   Of the old time and all their ancient heat
Of love could fail to stir her heart and bring
Her soul back to him with remembering

Nor could he think, still less, that she had proved
   False to her faith of her unfettered will ;
But rather deemed that she to it was moved
   By force or by some sad disloyal skill
   Of slander, that so many loves doth kill,—
And doubted not, in spite of all the let
Of years and duties, but she loved him yet.

For all the wealth of love bestowed on her
   And garnered up within his heart so long
Seemed surety to him that there yet must stir
   Some love in her, haply unknown, yet strong ;
   And as within the bird's throat sleeps the song,
Dumb for captivity, that yet the view
Of all his native woods would wake anew,

So, at his sight, he could not choose but deem,
   The old frank faith would wake in her afresh,
And like the tangles of some doubtful dream,
   She would shake off from her the weary mesh
   Of falseness,—and her eyes on his afresh
Rain love and truth, her lips once more rejoice
Him with the constant sweetness of her voice,

Renewing the dissevered bonds of love :
   And then the days of doubt should pass away
And be but as some mist that hangs above
   The certain summer of an August day,
   A little while, and tempers the sun-ray,—
And all the ancient bliss return to him,
A brighter noon because the dawn was dim.

Wherefore he set himself to haunt the ways
    Where she was wont to pass,—the market-place,
The square before the church on holidays,
    The paths tree-shadowed and the flower-set space
    Beside the river,—watching for her face
Morning and noon and night, as one in pain
Looks for the face of Death; but long in vain.

At length at the church door he met with her,
    Leant on her husband's arm and listening,
Well-pleased, to what he whispered.   Lovelier
    She seemed than her of his remembering
    Unto Girolamo; and a double sting
Ran through his heart, to look on her so fair
And know those fatal charms another's were.

By him, held dumb by hope and fear, she past,
    And by some hap, chancing to lift her eyes,
Straight on his face her starry glance she cast
    And looked at him a space; but in nowise '
    Her lover's form she seemed to recognise,
(Perchance for he was still with fever wan)
But saw him as a stranger, and passed on.

Full long, I ween, he deemed his death at hand,
   Being (it seemed) of his last hope deprived ;
But once again the expiring spark was fanned
   Into a flame, (so strong a hope is hived
   In lovers' breasts) and there once more revived
The wish of life in him, that he might prove
To end the doubtful fortune of his love.

For it might be (his hope 'gan whisper him)
   That she had looked on him and known him not,
Seeing he was so changed in face and limb
   By that fell fever, or some spell had got
   Empire on her, whereby she had forgot
The memory of their wooing and the face
Of him her lover, for a little space. ⌐

And if (as well he deemed that it might be)
   Some fatal charm were laid upon her sight,
He trusted to dispel that sorcery
   By prayers and offerings and the happy might
   Of counterspells ; and thus the sad despite
Of fortune foiled, she should possess again
Her memory, and take pity on his pain.

Wherefore by day and night long prayers he prayed
    To many a saint, and to that Lady bright,
That rules the skies, rich offerings he made
      To gain her grace, sparing not day or night
      To crave her intercession to relight
The old love in Salvestra, nor did cease
To wear her chapel's marble with his knees.

Nor did he trust alone in stress of prayer
    To break the sorcery of that opiate spell ;
But every occult influence did he dare,
      Invoking the divided powers of Hell
      To heal her blindness whom he loved so well,
Culling night-herbs, and on a scroll blood-writ
Burning strange cipherings beyond man's wit.

And then, at last, when every prayer was vain
    And no spell seemed to stand his hope in stead,
Seeing she passed him often and again
      And gave no sign of cognizance, but sped
      Upon her way with an averted head,
And not a word or look of hers exprest
Renewal of his image in her breast,

He would not even then lay hope aside,
   But comforted himself, despite his pain,
With the firm thought that there must needs abide
   Some memory of him within her brain,
   Which though his sight had failed to wake again,
(Being, as he was, so changed and strange to her)
The cadence of his speech should surely stir.

And so about within himself he cast
   How he should win to have her privately
To speak with him, proposing in this last
   Attempt to set his life upon the die ;
   But often as Salvestra passed him by
In streets or on the church's steps of stone,
He could not win to speak with her alone.

Wherefore, made bold by his supreme despair,
   He did resolve to seek her, spite of all,
Even in her husband's house, and being there,
   To make one last endeavour to recall
   Her love to him, whatever might befall ;
And if, alack ! his prayers should find no grace,
He might at least die looking on her face.

He knew her husband was a tent-maker
    And dwelt, with many others of his trade,
In a long street, that folk for many a year
    Called "Street of Tentmakers." At back there
       strayed
    The river; and between, long gardens made
A pleasaunce for the burghers, very fair
With tree-shade and the river running there.

Thither one afternoon he did betake
    Himself, what time the sultry Summer day
Grew faint and in the flower-beds and the brake
    The fierceness of the sunlight died away.
    Beneath a starry myrtle-bush he lay
And watched the glitter of the noon subside,
Across the running ripples of the tide.

And there, unseen, he waited, purposing,—
    When night was fallen on the scented air
And once the nightingales were waked to sing,—
    To make his secret way (if means there were
    And night were favouring and debonair)
Into Salvestra's chamber, and contrive
At least to speak with her once more alive.

Full wearily the unwilling day wore on :
   It seemed to him the light would never die :
Across the west like blood the sunset shone ;
   And to his sense, as sadly he did lie,
   The wafts of air seemed laden heavily
With incense for the dying, and the surg
Of ripples sounded like a funeral dirge.

At length the lagging daylight made an end
   Of gradual death ; and to the grateful night
He heard the sweet sound of the bells ascend
   From many a convent-steeple in his sight ;
   The dusky town put forth pale buds of light ;
He heard the throb of lute-strings, and afar
The silver chirp of some soft-swept guitar.

Then from his bed among the flowers he rose,
   And with the careless step of one who dares
A lawless act and heedeth not who knows,
   Being so sick at heart that nought he cares
   For aught that can befall him, up the stairs
Of stone he went and pushed against the door,
That swung ajar, yielding his hand before.

And entering, through the humble rooms he went,
   Noting the traces of Salvestra's hand,
That everywhere some grace of neatness lent
   To the poor dwelling.   Here, a little stand,—
   Wherein tall lilies, twined about a wand,
Hallowed the air with perfume,—there, the gold
And silver of the jasmine-blooms, enscrolled

About the little casement,—told their tale
   Of her sweet ministry ; and with each trace
Of her, fresh anguish did his heart assail,
   To think another's home possessed her grace,
   Another's hearth was lighted by her face .
And haply had he chanced her then to meet,
He might have fallen lifeless at her feet.

But all alone about the house he trod,
   And no one stayed, or asked him what he did ;
For so it chanced, Salvestra was abroad,
   With Paolo her husband.   Unforbid,
   He wandered sadly here and there, amid
The tokens of her presence, without aim,
Until into her bed-chamber he came.

There freshlier still the signs of her abode
    Did crowd on him; the ribbon that she wore
For festivals, the shining glass that showed
    Her eyes her beauty,—all the pretty store
    Of women's toys: and eke the table bore
A silver rose he gave her on its stem,
When love was in the summer-time for them.

The pretty bauble's sight brimmed up his eyes,
    At the sad thought that such a toy should keep
Its pristine brightness, when his Paradise
    And all the roses of his hope so deep
    In death did sleep the unremembering sleep;
And oft with many kisses did he press
That senseless relic of past happiness.

At last he heard a footstep on the stair,
    And ran to hide himself behind a heap
Of tent-cloths standing in a corner there,
    Thinking concealèd there himself to keep,
    Until, perchance, when Paolo should sleep,
He might come forth and gently her awake:
And haply she on him would pity take

Nor rouse her sleeping husband, but at worst
   Give ear to his sad pleading for the sake
Of all the gentle memories of erst :
   Mayhap, the cruel ice in her should break,
   And some soft pity at the least awake
In her, and she might speak some kindly word,
Which he might die more gladly having heard.

The chamber-door swung open, and she came,
   One hand about her husband's neck entwined ;
Whilst in the other hand, the taper's flame
   Leant to the lazy flutter of the wind :
   And as its flickering gleam upon her shined,
It seemed the amorous shade did strive for place
With the dim light, upon her lovely face.

The weary wight, tired with the sultry day
   And the long labour, on the couch flung down
His stalwart limbs, and soon asleep he lay :
   But she, unfastening her tresses' crown,
   Let down their sable flood, that all did drown
Her form, until she gathered them again
And set her to comb out each silken skein.

Lingering awhile before her glass she stood,
   Joying to look upon her lovely face,
And with a musing sweet content reviewed
   The perfect harmony of every grace :
   Then, with unhasting hands, each envious lace
She did unloose, that bound her body fair,
And stood all naked in her floating hair.

Ah ! not for me her loveliness to sing
   And the rich sweetness of each pearly limb !
My song would droop its slow and faltering wing,
   Did I enforce its weakness to that hymn
   Of silver splendours or my pen to limn
The sweet snows of her breast and the delight
Of her clear body's symphony of white.

I would I could command his lyre of gold,
   That sang that Marie loved of Chastelard,
Or his full harp, that of fair Nyssia told,
   Guarding her jealous beauty like a star,
   Or else his silver lute, whose ladies are
Florise and Cypris and that Goddess bright
That leads the silver lapses of the night.

Alas ! my heart is sore for his despite
   That saw his love, that never should be his,
Then first unveil her beauties to his sight !
   It was as if before some soul, that is
   In flames of hell, a dream of heaven's bliss
Were conjured up to mock his anguished sense
And make his thought of horror more intense.

He would have called to her,—but could nor speak
   Nor move; it seemed some strange and fettering
      swoon
Compelled his sense, so sick he was and weak
   With waste desire. Till she put off her shoon,
   And covering the lamp let in the moon,
That filled the chamber with its argent tide ;
Then laid her by her sleeping husband's side.

Now was the hour at hand when he should prove
   The last device of his resolved despair :
And yet awhile he could not win to move,
   But gazed full long upon her sleeping there,
   Pillowed within a fragrant cloud of hair,
With parted lips and heaving breasts, that shone
Like lilies on a lake by moonlight wan.

At last he did shake off the numbing spell
   That held his sense in bonds of stirlessness ;
And from his place he crept with feet that fell
   As noiselessly as fairies' feet that press
   The dewdrop grass. The room was shadowless ;
Her husband slept the heavy sleep of toil ;
And the void lamp had wasted all its oil.

Upon his knees beside the bed he sank,
   As one that kneels before a virgin shrine,
And with long looks of yearning sadness drank
   Her lovely sight. All bathed in white moonshine,
   Stirless she lay ; and on her lidded eyne
Such peace abode, one might have deemed it death,
Save for the fluttering witness of her breath.

At length, with tremulous touch and wavering,
   His hand he laid upon her ivory breast,
That for a moment stayed its fluttering
   And throbbed uneasily, as if opprest :
   But yet therefore ceased not Salvestra's rest ;
So feather-light his tender touch did lie,
She did but flutter out a gentle sigh.

Then, bending o'er the cover of the bed,
  He set his lips upon her sleep-sealed eyes
And eke upon her mouth's twin flowers of red,
  As softly as a fallen flower, that lies
  And floats upon a river, lily-wise.
Still did she sleep; and he, grown bolder still,
Of clinging kisses took his thirsty fill.

Ah, when was lover true yet satisfied
  With lover's food of kisses warm and sweet?
He would have kissed and kissed, until there died
  The life in him; but, as his lips did meet
  And clung to hers more close, the sudden heat
Quickened the throbbing pulses of her heart
And forced the ivory gates of sleep apart.

Her heavy lids drew up and loosed the light
  Captive within their envious prison-sleep;
And as his kneeling figure met her sight,
  The drowsy sweetness, that her eyes did steep,
  Into a pretty fearfulness did leap;
And for her sheer affright she would have cried,
But in her throat the words sank down and died.

For in his face, bent down towards her own,
  The lamp of such a perfect love was lit,
And in his sad clear eyes the peace alone
  Of such a loveful gentleness was writ,
  She could not seek for any fear in it,
But lay and looked on him, with still surprise
Rounding the sleepy sweetness of her eyes.

Then, "Sleepest thou, my love of loves?" he said :
  And at his voice, the thoughts, that in her breast
Had for long absence and the years lain dead,
  Upon her in a crowd of memories prest.
  Like birds returning to their last year's nest,
The words and deeds of the sweet time of yore
Rose up and lived before her thought once more.

And with the memory, such a fretful tide
  Of struggling fancies did oppress her brain,
That for relief aloud she would have cried
  And help ; but as to speak she strove in vain,
  He spoke once more and prayed her to refrain,
For 'twas Girolamo, whom she had loved,
In the old days, alas ! so far removed.

Then with soft words to her he did recall
    The linked delight of those unsullied days,
When each to each was lovers' all in all
    And wrought with other in Love's pleasant praise,
    Heart joined to heart ; and in all tender ways
Love could contrive to work upon her grace,
He did entreat her fairly to retrace

The vanished paths of faith, to turn aside
    From the deceitful ways in which her feet
Had lately wandered,—since false lips had lied
    Surely to her of him,—and once more greet,
    With those long looks of love that were so sweet,
His thirsty eyes, that had of her fair sight
Bereavèd been so many a day and night.

And with full many a piteous device
    He strove to turn her heart again to him
And conjure back the lovelight in her eyes,
    Recounting how when absence was so grim
    And sad to him, her face had ne'er grown dim
Within his memory, but clear and fair,
The thought of her was with him everywhere.

And how all fairest ladies of the land,
 Where damozels are loveliest, had failed
To move the heart he left within her hand,
 And how no pleasant sight or sport prevailed
 To win his thought to gladness, that bewailed,
'Mid proudest feast and music's silveriest swell,
His banishment from her he loved so well.

Nor did he fail to paint his great despair
 And all the springs of life dried up and waste,
And how for him thenceforth no thing was fair
 Enough, no joy of living could he taste,
 That might retain his weary soul, in haste
To break the chains of that abhorrent earth,
Her love alone made fair and worship-worth.

For of a surety (and he showed his face,
 Wan-white with sickness, and his sunken eyes,)
The life should linger in its weary place
 Small time after the new day's sun should rise,
 Unless her hand reknit the severed ties,
That to his spirit only peace could give,
And her lips' honey lent him strength to live.

So he poured prayers into her listening ears;
  And all the while her hand in his he held,
Bathing its ivory with the bitter tears,
  That from his breast so thick and fiercely welled,
  That now and then to pause he was compelled;
And as he ceased, upon her hand he poured
Kisses more eloquent than any word.

And for awhile it seemed to him, the strength
  Of his despair prevailed upon her soul;
For her lids quivered, and adown the length
  Of her soft cheek a silver tear did roll,
  And a half sigh out of her bosom stole;
And as upon her hand his lips he prest,
He heard the heart throb loudly in her breast.

Alas! his hope was all in vain. Full soon
  She drew her hand out from between his own,
And trembling, as one waking from a swoon,
  Conjured him, for God's sake, to get him gone
  And leave her quiet—else she were undone:
For of a truth the day was near to break,
And momently her husband might awake.

" For in those ancient foolish days," she said,
    " We were but girl and boy, and in child-guise
Did use to kiss and toy with each, and played
    At love and courtship, for no harm might rise
    Of such child's sport : but now 'tis otherwise ;
For years have passed away since that befell,
And I am married, as thou knowest well.

" And ill it should become me to the love
    Of any other man to give consent
Than this my husband ; wherefore, if there move
    Within thee any fear of God or saint,
    I do entreat thee now to be content
With that which thou has dared and done to night,
And get thee gone before the day grow white.

" For but consider what a cruel wrong
    Would fall on me through thine unmeasured heat,
And how the harm to me would be life-long,
    If day should come and find thee at my feet.
    Now is my life happy and calm and sweet ;
For Paolo my husband loves me well,
And in content and peace with him I dwell.

"But if by evil chance he should awake
   And see thee kneeling thus by my bedside,
He would leave loving me for thy rash sake,
   And all my happy days with strife be tried ;
   So that no more in peace I could abide
With him,—even if no other harm ensue :
Wherefore, I pray thee, this I ask thee, do.

"Or if the thought of ill to hap to me
   Avail not to avert thy wanton will,
Bethink thee that no hope can ever be
   That any act of mine shall aye fulfil
   Thy mad desire, or that there lingers still
A spark of love for thee within my heart.
Thanks thou shalt have, if but thou wilt depart."

Ah me, what misery can equal his,
   That loves and hears his dearest love confess,
With that sweet voice that conjures back old bliss,
   The sad impeach of cold forgetfulness !
   I wot there is no pang of hell nor stress
Of endless death, that can prevail above
The wistfulness of unrequited love !

So knelt Girolamo,—and listening
   To those cold words from that belovèd mouth,
That did close up for him the gates of Spring
   And all the golden memories of youth,
   Knew all his hope in vain and felt the growth
Of that cold bringer of the eternal Rest
Stir in the silent chambers of his breast.

But even while he felt the chills of Death
   Creep through his heart, he could not choose but
      take,
(So strong is Love, and such charm lingereth
   About the loved one's presence !) whilst she spake,
   Some sad delight. Even though his heart should
      break
At her harsh words, the sweetness of her voice
Could not but make his faithful soul rejoice.

But when she ceased the music of her speech,
   The spell dissolved from him, and he awoke
Unto his full despair nor did beseech
   Her any more nor strove again to evoke
   The phantom of dead love. The heavy stroke
Was merciful, and did benumb his brain,
So that he thought no more to strive in vain

Nor did he find it in him to upbraid
   Her cruelty; but with a weary air
And a sad voice, that might not be gainsaid,
   He did entreat of her one little prayer
   Of his to grant and lighten his despair;—
That she would let him in the couch, beside
Her body warm, a little while abide;—

For all the heat had left him, with the chill
   Of the night-air,—and swore to her to lie
Silent by her nor touch her, but quite still
   And mute to bide the while;—and presently
   (He did avouch) before the day drew nigh,
As soon as he regained a little heat,
He would arise and go with noiseless feet.

Then she,—some little moved by his despair
   And haply thinking thus the quicklier
To be relieved of him,—unto his prayer
   Consented and did let him lie by her,
   Enjoining him to lie and never stir,
And when as she should bid him go, that he
Should rise and get him gone immediately.

But he, his weary body being laid
  Within the bed, began to ponder o'er
Within himself the things that she had said ;
  And in his thought revolving all the sore
  Sad end of every pleasant thing of yore,
And all the grief that in his heart did lie,
He presently resolved himself to die.

So, with one last fond look at her sweet face,
  That lay beside him with averted eyes,
And one last prayer to Mary full of grace
  And one last Ave intermixed with sighs,
  He folded up his hands to sleep, childwise,
And by his dearly-loved Salvestra's side,
He rendered up his gentle soul and died.

So lay Girolamo the while the hours
   Slid onwards through the cloisters of the dusk :
And now the day began to put forth flowers,
   Pale buds of morning opening from the husk
   Of the small hours ; and all the lights, that busk
The cheerless heavens in the earliest dawn,
Grew grey and chill across each Eastern lawn.

And as the earliest dawn-streak in the East
   Began to glimmer through the casement's glass,
Salvestra started from her fitful rest ;
   And gradually, what had come to pass
   That night recalling to her mind, " Alas !
The dusk is burning to the break of day,"
She said, "and yet Girolamo doth stay !"

Then did she chide him for his broken word
   And did conjure him rise without delay
And get him gone.   Yet not a whit he stirred,
   But dumb and motionless as death he lay
   And gave no heed to aught that she could say ;
Till she, supposing him with sleep opprest,
Stretched out her hand and touched him on the
      breast.

But lo ! her passing hand aroused him not ;
 And to her touch, as cold as any ice
His bosom smote.   A deadly terror got
 A sudden hold upon her.   Twice or thrice
 She called him by his name.   Then did she rise,
And bending o'er him, felt no stir of breath
Nor throb of pulse, and knew that it was death.

Then such a deathly fear laid hands on her,
 And such an icy coldness of dismay,
That for awhile she could nor speak nor stir ;
 But by the dead all tremblingly she lay ;
 Whilst through the clouds the grey and early day
Crept from the casement to the dead man's place
And threw a ghastly light upon his face.

Then gradually the thoughts began to take
 Some form in her ; and she was sore afraid
Lest Paolo her husband should awake
 And find a lifeless man beside her laid ;
 For much she feared lest he should her upbraid,
Seeing the grisly sight would surely move
The man to deem her faithless to his love.

And in her thought awhile considering
   How she should best avert the blame she feared,
At last she did resolve to tell the thing
   Unto her husband as a story heard
   In idle talk or else a chance occurred
To other unknown folk, and so to know
Whether the thing should anger him or no.   ,

Then waking him, as if by accident
   She did relate to him how, in a dream,
So strange and sad a thing to her was sent,
   That still before her mind's eye it did seem
   To be presented, and (as she did deem)
Till she had told him all, it would not cease
To weary her, or leave her any peace.

Then, in ambiguous words (concealing nought
   Save name and place) the fatal circumstance
Of all the ills to that sad loveling wrought
   By love, she told him,—how a youth did chance
   To love a maid, and being sent to France,
After two years returned and found her wed,—
And how, in his despair, beside her bed

By night he knelt ; and finding every prayer
　　For love's renewal vain, did beg to be
Allowed to warm himself from the cold air
　　A little by her side　To which prayer she,
　　Moved by his grief to pity, did agree ;
And how, when he had lain awhile and said
No word, she had awoke and found him dead.

And as she made an end of saying this,
　　She prayed that he would tell her, of his mind,
Whether the wife therein had done amiss,
　　And what the husband, who awoke to find
　　A stark dead man beside his wife reclined,
Should do.　Whereto he answered, that the man
Must hold her blameless, since, as woman can,

She had resisted all her lover's suit ;
　　But that, before the folk began to go
About the ways, whilst yet the streets were mute,
　　He should, to avert the evils that might grow
　　From slanderous tongues—if any came to know
The thing—take up the dead, and through the town
Bearing him, in his doorway lay him down.

Whereat Salvestra, being lightened much
  At heart to hear him speak his mind so fair
And righteous, took his hand and made him touch
  Girolamo his bosom lying there
  Stark dead and cold ; whereby he was aware
She had made known to him, in other's name,
Her own mischance.   Yet not a word of blame

To her he said, but rather comforted
  Her timorous soul and bade her have no care.
Then rising straight he lifted up the dead ;
  And on his shoulders through the streets he bare
  Girolamo's sad body to the stair
Before his mother's palace in the town ;
And there all reverently he laid it down.

Now when the day was wakened with the sun
    And men began about the streets to go,
One of the Countess' servants saw her son
    Lie as asleep within the portico,
    And touching him, to know if it were so,
Found that the life from its sad seat had fled,
And told his mistress that her son was dead.

Then she, for pride repressing her despair,
    Shed not a tear ; but with a pale set face,
Commanded instantly that they should bear
    The body to the chief church of the place
    And set it by the Virgin's altar space,
That there all due observances might be
Filled, as behoved his rank and ancestry.

So with the majesty of funeral rites,
   They bore Girolamo into the fane;
And there, amid a blaze of votive lights,
   They set his senseless body down again;
    And with full many a prayer and many a strain
Of ceremonial song, they did commend
His soul to God : nor did they make an end

Of mourning him ; but as the manner is,
   When any noble dies, they did bewail
His piteous death and loss of earthly bliss
   In earliest youth : and soon the sorry tale
    Of all his heavy fortune did not fail
To stir among the people gathered there
And move their hearts to pity his despair.

Now, when the news was come to Paolo,
   Girolamo his body had been found,
Most earnestly he did desire to know
   What talk might be among the folk around,
    And to what cause—seeing there was no wound
Upon the man nor of disease a sign—
His strange and sudden death they did assign.

And to this end, Salvestra he enjoined
　To mingle with the women at the door,
Within the church, and hear what tale was coined
　Among the folk, and thus herself assure
　That he had been unnoticed—when he bore
The body home—of any citizen:
And he would do the like among the men.

The thing he bade was pleasing unto her,
　For (such a doubtful thing is woman's mind)
The pity that his love had failed to stir
　Within her bosom, while the Fates were kind,
　Possessed her now; and she, that could not find
A gentle word to gladden him alive,
Felt for the dead the ancient love revive.

So with a trembling step she bent her way
　Towards the church; and when afar she saw
The dead man's face across the dense array,
　Love took revenge of his contemnèd law,*
　And such invincible desire did draw
Her feet towards the place where he was laid,
She rested not until her way she made

* " Amor ch' a null' amato amar perdona."—DANTE.

Athwart the crowd and stood beside the bier ;
  Then with a haggard eye considering
The sad sweet face furrowed with many a tear
  And worn and wasted sore with sorrowing,
  The thought of his despair prevailed to bring
To pass what all his life had failed to impart,
And Love gat hold upon her stubborn heart.

Awhile she stood, with haggard straining eyes
  And hands that seemed to stretch towards the dead,
As if to conjure back from Paradise
  The gentle soul from the sad body fled ;
  Silent she stood, and not a tear she shed :
But her face bent towards him more and more,
And her drooped knees sank slowly to the floor.

At last her swelling bosom found a vent
  For all its weight of anguish and despair ;
And with a cry that all the silence rent
  And stirred the calling echoes far and near,
  She fell upon his bosom, lying there,
And kissed the cold lips and the death-sealed eyes
And called upon him madly to arise.

For Death could surely have no power on him,
 Seeing she loved him with so fierce a heat ;
Her kiss should surely from the very rim
 Of the black night recall his wandering feet.
 But none the less the white face cold and sweet
Lay passionless, the pale lips answered not,
And all her blandishments availed no jot.

Then gradually, seeing that in vain
 Her tardy kindness came, nor all love's stress
Availed her to reknit life's severed skein,
 She did abate for very weariness
 Her idle strife and lay all motionless:
But still with one long kiss her hot lips clave
To his cold mouth that none in answer gave.

And thus awhile she lay, her haggard face
 Pressed unto his that died for love of her,
Whilst on the floor her locks did interlace
 With the full golden clusters of his hair.
 Long time she lay on him and did not stir ;
And on the air there hung a ghastly spell
Of silence, measured by the tolling bell.

At length, the pitying folk that stood around
　　And wept for dolour of that piteous sight,
Thinking Salvestra fallen of a swound,
　　Would have uplifted from the marble white
　　Her senseless form ; but when they brought to light
Her lovely face, they found the sweet soul fled
And knew these lovers for waste love lay dead.

So Death took pity on ill-fortuned love
　　And at the last did grant these lovers twain
That boon all other earthly bliss above,
　　At rest beside each other to be lain
　　And never stir from their embrace again.
Ah Love ! thou art full sweet ; but never yet
Did any man of thee such guerdon get !

And there they buried them beneath the trees,
　　Beside the running river, breast to breast,
These two sad lovers.　Ladies, if it please
　　Your gentle hearts to hear of folk opprest
　　Of love, I pray you use it softliest,
This little song of mine, and say with me,
God save all gentle souls that lovers be.

Ah me! shall Love for ever suffer wrong?
Shall none avail to stay the steps of Fate?
Since Summer and its roses and the song
Of choiring birds are powerless to abate
The conquering curse, the uncompassionate;
But all themselves must seek that frozen shore
Where Spring and all its flowers have gone before.

Alas! meseems there is none other thing
Assured to us that work and watch and weep,
Save only memory and sorrowing
And the soft lapse into the eternal sleep!
The harvest that we sow, what hands shall reap,
What eyes shall see the glories that we dream,
What ears shall throb unto the songs we deem,

We know not; nor the end of love is sure,
(Alas! how much less sure than anything!)
   Whether the little love-light shall endure
In the clear eyes of her we loved in Spring,
Or if the faint flowers of remembering
   Shall blow, we know not: only this we know,—
   Afar Death comes with silent steps and slow.

Men lay their lives before the feet of Love,
   Strewing his way with many-coloured flowers,
And poets use to set his praise above
   All other rulers of the days and hours:
   From age to age untold, recurrent showers
Of psalm and song attest his empery
And crown him God above all Gods that be.

   And with an equal breath, on that dark Lord
That rules the going out from life and light,
   The hate and fear of men have been outpoured,
In words that borrowed blackness from the night;
Nor have the singers spared with songs to smite
   His silent head, styling him bitterest foe
   Of that fair God that myrtle-crowned doth go.

And yet, what Love could not prevail to do,
Companied round with every goodly thought
And every happy chance that men ensue,
When all his charms of flowers and birdsongs wrought
And all his sorceries availèd nought
To give these lovers peace and twinned delight,—
That Death wrought out of his unaided might.

And thou, O best-belovèd of the sad,
O Death, the angel of the end of tears!
Let those heap blame on thee, whose lives are glad,
For whom thy dwelling is the dusk of fears.
I praise thee, that have loved thee many years:
Though men revile thee, thou art dear to me:
Sad is my song; I bring it all to thee.

For me, I love thee not for lives beyond
The compassed darkness of the accomplished Fate;
I look not, I, with dazzled eyes and fond,
To find new worlds behind thine iron gate;
I love thee for thyself compassionate;
I seek thee not for heavens and new life,
Only for thine embrace that shuts out strife.

I look not, I, for the awakening,
After long sleep, in brighter worlds to come ;
* I look but for the end of wearying,*
For pain to cease and sorrow to be dumb ;
To lay me down, with stricken sense and numb,
* Hiding my weary face within thy breast,*
* Rest in thy bosom, and around thee rest.*

But you, my Masters, in whose mighty track
* I have ensued with slow and faltering feet,*
I will crave pardon of you, if I lack,
* In this my song, to follow on the beat*
* Of your firm footsteps—if my errant heat*
Have, in the sad enchantment of my days,
Put off the strong assurance of your lays !

And first, glad Master, standing with one foot
On earth, and one foot in the Faery land—
* Whose song, with virgin Una taking root,*
Branches, a forest-tree majestic, spanned
From earth through heaven unto the elfin strand—
* Thou that didst count the seasons and the hours*
* With the fair forest calendar of flowers,*

That knew'st no sadness, building up thy song
With love and life and deeds of high emprise,
That rod'st with cheerful heart the world along,
Counting to crown fair life with Paradise—
I pray thee, Master fair and glad and wise,
To pardon me, if none of these I seek;
For I am sad, alas ! and very weak.

And thou, O star-browed singer—folded round
With the vague awe of the Invisible,
As with a cloak—whose radiant front is crowned
With triple coronals, fair and terrible,
Attesting the assay of heaven and hell—
Thou, whose aspèct indeed is very sad,
Yet therewithin the hope of heaven had

Burns like a glory and a shining fire—
O pilgrim of the high celestial town,
Forgive my weakling thought, if it aspire
Not to the palm-branch and the starry crown—
Only the soft rest and the lying down
To dreamless sleep and cease of sorrowing;
For I am weak and ask a little thing.

A little thing, a narrow sorry hope!
Indeed a little thing to look upon,
*   If one be glad and in the Future's scope*
Long vistas of fair places to be won
And valorous deeds for doing follow on,—
*   A weary hope, i' faith, if one be strong*
*   And run the race in gladness and with song.*

But if the life be grief in any one
*   And his despair shrink from the face of light,*
Fearing to see the splendour of the sun—
*   If day for sadness wither in his sight*
*   And his tears fill the watches of the night,*
If love be madness and the hope of men
Seem to his soul a mockery,—ah then

*   He cares not to renew the weariness*
Of unspent life within the years unknown;
*   He shall not seek the never-ending stress*
Of the sad days for him immortal grown—
A palace where his soul shall walk alone;
*   His heart aspires but to the end of pain,*
*   The sleep where morning never comes again.*

And thus I hail thee, Lord of all my lays !
  Master and Healer, coming with soft wing !
I lift my feeble voice unto thy praise,
    For thou to me art hope in every thing.
    Others have glory and remembering,
Fair hope of future life and crown of faith,
Love and delight ; but I, I have but death.

  Wherefore I praise thee, seeing thou alone,
Of all things underneath the heavens born,
    Art all assured. For is it not unknown
Whether the gold sun on another morn
Shall glitter, or the Spring come to adorn
    Once more the woods and fields with winter pale ?
    This but we know, Thou Death shalt never fail !

And unto thee I bring this weakling song,
  (For I am thine, and all my little skill)
Wherein, alone among the busy throng,
    I have enforced me sadly to fulfil
    My meed of thanks to thee,—and loudlier still
My growing voice shall praise thee, Death, than now,
Lord of the Future, certain only thou !

18—2

VILLANELLE.

(With a copy of Swinburne's Poems and Ballads, Second Series.)

THE thrush's singing days are fled
His heart is dumb for love and pain :
The nightingale shall sing instead.

Too long the wood-bird's heart hath bled
With love and dole at every vein :
The thrush's singing days are fled.

The music in his breast is dead,
His soul will never flower again :
The nightingale shall sing instead.

Love's rose has lost its early red,
The golden year is on the wane ;
The thrush's singing days are fled.

The years have beaten down his head,
He's mute beneath the winter's rain :
The nightingale shall sing instead.

Hard use hath snapped the golden thread
Of all his wild-wood songs in twain ;
The thrush's singing days are fled.

His voice is dumb for drearihead :
What matters it?   In wood and lane
The nightingale shall sing instead.

Dear, weary not for what is sped.
What if, for stress of heart and brain,
The thrush's singing days are fled ;
The nightingale shall sing instead.

CINQUAINS.

I STROVE to hide the load that Love on me did
    lay :
In vain ; and sleep from me for aye is fled away.
Since that wanhope doth press my heart both night
    and day,
I cry aloud "O Fate, hold back thy hand, I pray !
    For all my soul is sick for anguish and dismay."

If that the Lord of Love were just indeed to me,
Sleep had not fled my eyes by his unkind decree.
Have pity, sweet, on one that is for love of thee
Worn out and wasted sore, that once was rich and
    free,
    Now humbled and cast down by Love from his
    array.

Thy foes cease not to speak thee ill; I heed not, I :
But stop my ears to them and give them back the lie :
I'll keep my troth with her I love, until I die.
" Thou lovest one estranged," they say ; and I reply
   " Enough ; fate blinds the eyes of those that are
     its prey."

II.

Who says to thee " The first of love is free,"
Tell him, " Not so ; but on the contrary ;
'Tis all constraint, wherein no blame can be.
History, indeed, attests this verity ;
   It does not style the good coin falsified.

Say, if thou wilt, " The taste of pain is sweet,
Or to be spurned by Fortune's flying feet ; "
Talk of whatever makes the heart to beat
For grief or gladness, fortune or defeat ;
   'Twixt hope and fear I tarry stupefied.

But as for him whose happy days are light,
Fair maids whose lips with smiles are ever bright,
Sweet with the fragrant breath of their delight,
Who has his will, unhindered of despite,
   'Tis not with him that craven fear should bide.

From the Arabic.

LOVE'S AUTUMN.

(Field's Nocturne in D Minor.)

YES, love, the Spring shall come again;
    But not as once it came :
Once more in meadow and in lane
    The daffodils shall flame,
The cowslips blow, but all in vain :
    Alike, yet not the same.

The roses that we plucked of old
    Were dewed with heart's delight :
Our gladness steeped the primrose-gold
    In half its lovely light :
The hopes are long since dead and cold,
    That flushed the wind-flowers' white.

Ah, who shall give us back our Spring ?
    What spell can fill the air
With all the birds of painted wing

That sang for us whilere?
What charm reclothe with blossoming
　　Our lives grown blank and bare?

What sun can draw the ruddy bloom
　　Back to hope's faded rose?
What stir of summer re-illume
　　Our hearts' wreckt garden-close?
What flowers can fill the empty room
　　Where now the nightshade grows?

'Tis but the Autumn's chilly sun
　　That mocks the glow of May;
'Tis but the pallid bindweeds run
　　Across our garden way,
Pale orchids, scentless every one,
　　Ghosts of the summer day.

Yet, if it must be so, 'tis well:
　　What part have we in June?
Our hearts have all forgot the spell
　　That held the summer noon;
We echo back the cuckoo's knell,
　　And not the linnet's tune.

What should we do with roses now,
　　Whose cheeks no more are red?
What violets should deck our brow,
　　Whose hopes long since are fled?
Recalling many a wasted vow
　　And many a faith struck dead.

Bring heath and pimpernel and rue,
　　The Autumn's sober flowers:
At least their scent will not renew
　　The thought of happy hours
Nor drag sad memory back unto
　　That lost sweet time of ours.

Faith is no sun of summer-tide,
　　Only the pale calm light
That, when the Autumn clouds divide,
　　Hangs in the watchet height,—
A lamp, wherewith we may abide
　　The coming of the night.

And yet, beneath its languid ray,
　　The moorlands bare and dry
Bethink them of the summer day

And flower, far and nigh,
With fragile memories of the May,
   Blue as the August sky.

These are our flowers : they have no scent
   To mock our waste desire,
No hint of bygone ravishment
   To stir the faded fire :
The very soul of sad content
   Dwells in each azure spire.

I have no violets : you laid
   Your blight upon them all :
It was your hand, alas ! that made
   My roses fade and fall,
Your breath my lilies that forbade
   To come at summer's call.

Yet take these scentless flowers and pale,
   The last of all my year :
Be tender to them ; they are frail :
   But if thou hold them dear,
I'll not their brighter kin bewail,
   That now lie cold and sere.

ASPECT AND PROSPECT.

Jam-i-mäi, khoun-i-dil, her yek be-kesé dadend.—HAFIZ.
Every man hath his gift, one a cup of wine, another heart's
blood.

I.

THE time is sad with many a sign and token;
   Desire and doubting in all hearts have met;
The ancient orders of the world are broken;
   The night is spent, the morning comes not yet:
   Men go with face against the Future set,
Each asking each, "When shall the wreak be wroken?
When shall the God come and the word be spoken
   To end Life's passion and its bloody sweat?"

For sowing time hath failed us even at reaping;
   Time hath torn out the eyes and heart of faith;
Of all our gladness there remaineth weeping;
   Of all our living we have woven us death:

For many a hope is dead for lack of breath,
And many a faith hath fallen and is sleeping,
Weary to death with the long hopeless keeping
   The watch for day that never morroweth.

For all our lives are worn with hopeless yearning;
   There is no pleasantness in all our days :
The world is waste, and there is no returning
   For our tired feet into old flowered ways.
   Long use hath shorn our summer of its rays ;
Of all our raptures there is left but burning ;
We are grown sadly wise, and for discerning
   The sweet old dreams are hueless to our gaze.

We trust not Love, for he is God no longer :
   Another hath put on his pleasant guise :
The greater God hath bowed him to the stronger ;
   Death looks at life from many a lover's eyes :
   And underneath the linden-tree he lies,
The gracious torch-bearer of ancient story,
His sweet face faded, and his pinions' glory
   Dim as the gloss of grass-grown memories.

No gods have we to trust to, new or olden ;
   The blue of heaven knows their thrones no more :
The races of the gods in death are holden :
   Their pale ghosts haunt the icy river's shore :
   Availeth not our beating at their door :
There is no presence in their halls beholden ;
The silence fills their jewelled thrones and golden ;
   The shadow lies along their palace-floor.

And lo ! if any set his heart to singing,
   Thinking to witch the world with love and light,
Strains of old memories set the stern chords ringing ;
   The morning answers with the songs of night :
   For who can sing of pleasance and delight,
When all the sadness of the world is clinging
About his heart-strings, and each breeze is bringing
   Its burden of despairing and despite.

Help is there none : night covers us down-lying
   To sleep that comes at last with devious dreams ;
The morning brings us sadness but and sighing :
   We gather sorrow from the noontide beams :

And if a man set eyes on aught that seems
An oasis of peace, he finds on nighing
Its promise false, and sad almost to dying
    Turns from the mirage and its treacherous streams.

II.

And yet one hope by well-nigh all is cherished,—
Albeit many hold it unconfest,—
The dream of days that, when this life has perished
And all its strife and turmoil are at rest,
Shall rise for men out of some mystic West,—
A paradise of peace, where death comes never
And life flows calmly as some dreamy river
That wanders through the islands of the Blest :

A dream of love-lorn hearts made whole of sorrow,
Of all life's doubts and puzzles solved for aye,
Of severed lives reknit in one to-morrow
Of endless bliss beneath the cloudless sky ;
A dream of lands where hope shall never die,
But in the fair clear fields, browbound with moly,
Our dead desires shall wander, healed and holy,
And over all a mystic peace shall lie ;

A peace that shall be woven of old sadness
And bitter memories grown honey-sweet,
Where our lost hopes shall live again in gladness,
Chaining the summer to their happy feet ;
Where never fulness with desire shall meet,
Nor the sweet earth divide from the clear heaven,
Nor mortal grossness shall avail to leaven
The ecstasy of that supernal seat.

III.

Ah ! lovely dreams that come and go !
Shall ever hope to harvest grow ?
    Of all that sow shall any reap ?
I know not, I : but this I know,
Whether the years bring weal or woe,
    Whether the Future laugh or weep,
    I shall not heed it,—I shall sleep.

I have lived out this life of ours ;
I can no more.—Through shine and showers,
   March lapses into full July :
The May sun coaxes out the floweis,
And through the splendid summer hours
    Their tender little lives go by,
    And when the winter comes, they die.

But in the Spring they live again.
Not so with us, whose lives have lain
   In ways where love and pain are rife,—
Whose seventy years of sadness strain
Towards the gates of rest in vain ;
    Our souls are worn with doubt and strife ;
    We have no seed of second life.

And yet for those whose lives have been
Through storm and sun alike serene,
   Drinking the sunshine and the dew
In every break of summer sheen,—
I doubt not but the unforeseen
    May treasure for these flower-like few
    A life where heart and soul renew ;

A life where Love no more shall bring
The pains of hell upon its wing,
   Where perfect peace at least shall dwell,—
That happy peace that is the King
Of all the goods we poets sing,—
   That all with aching hearts foretell,
   Yet know them unattainable.

But we, whom Love hath wrecked and torn,
Whose lives with waste desire are worn,—
   Whose souls life-long have been as lyres
Vibrating to each breath that's borne
Across our waste of days forlorn,—
   Whose paths are lit with funeral fires,
   The monuments of dead desires,—

We, for whom many lives have past,
Through storm and summer, shine and blast,
   Within our one man's span of years,—
We may not hope for peace at last
Save where the shade of Sleep is cast,
   And from our eyes Death's soft hand clears
   The thought alike of smiles and tears.

Yet (for we loved you, brothers all,—
That love us not,—despite the wall
   Of crystal that between us lies)
We, to whose eyes, whate'er befall,
No angel could the hope recall,
   We dream for you of brighter skies,
   Of life new-born in Paradise.

We hope for you that golden day
When God (alas !) shall wipe away
   The tears from all the eyes that weep ;
And from our lonely lives we pray
That, of that happy time, some ray
   Of your filled hope, your souls that reap,
   May reach us, dream-like, in our sleep.

MELISANDE.

A H, lady of the lands of gold !
   Who shall lay hands on thee and hold
    Thy beauty for a space as long
    As pausing of a linnet's song ?
Ah, lady of the lays of old,
   When love is life and right is wrong !

Ah, lady of the dear old dream !
We watch Love's roses on the stream
    That spins its silver in the land
    Where garlands glitter from thy hand :
Ah, singer of the sweets that seem !
   When shall the dream take shape and stand ?

Ah, dear in dreams, lost long ago !
A sound of lutings soft and low,
  A scent of roses newly prest,
  Cease never from the dreamful West :
When shall a man draw near to know
  The sweetness of thy perfect breast ?

II.

A dream of days too far to fill :
The thin clear babble of the rill
  That trickles through the fainting flowers ;
  A monotone of mourning hours ;
The dim dawn coming sad and still ;
  The evening's symphony of showers.

A lone land under a sere sky ;
And, stretching towards the veil on high,
  My soul, a flower that seeks the sun ;
  The dull days dropping, one by one ;
The darkness drawing ever nigh ;
  And still nor dream nor life is won.

III.

Ah sunflower-heart ! ah Melisande !
When shall the dream take shape and stand ?
    When shall thy lips melt into mine ?
    When shall I drink thy looks like wine ?
Shall earth for once turn fairy-land
    And all the past take shape and shine ?

Alas ! such hopes were vain indeed !
The waste world knoweth not the seed
    That bears the blossom of delight :
    Shall one go forth to sow the night
And look to reap sun-coloured weed
    And lilies of the morning light ?

Who would not be content to know
That at the last,—when sin and woe
    Had done their worst, and life were lain
    Before the gates that shut out pain,—
The bitter breeze of death should blow
    The mirage from the sullen plain,

And for a little sun-filled space
His sight should feed on his love's face,
   And in her eyes his soul drink deep,—
   And then upon him death should creep
And snatch him, sudden, to the place
   Where all things gather to a sleep !

Ah lovers, God but grant you this,—
To breathe your life out in a kiss,
   To sleep upon your lady's breast
   The hour life lapses into rest !
For me, I ask no other bliss
   Than Rudel's, deeming his the best.

THE END.

A NEW TRAGEDY

BY

R. H. HORNE,

AUTHOR OF 'ORION,' 'THE DEATH OF MARLOWE,' ETC., ETC.

ENTITLED

LAURA DIBALZO;

OR,

THE PATRIOT MARTYRS.

𝔇𝔢𝔡𝔦𝔠𝔞𝔱𝔢𝔡 𝔱𝔬 𝔱𝔥𝔢 𝔦𝔩𝔩𝔲𝔰𝔱𝔯𝔦𝔬𝔲𝔰 𝔐𝔢𝔪𝔬𝔯𝔶 𝔬𝔣

WASHINGTON,

AND TO THE EQUALLY PURE PATRIOTIC NAMES OF

KOSCIUSKO,   KOSSUTH,

MAZZINI,   GARIBALDI.

NEWMAN AND CO.,
43, HART STREET, BLOOMSBURY, W.C.

MR. PAYNE'S WORKS.

———oo⫶o⫶oo———

1. THE MASQUE OF SHADOWS and other Poems.

2. INTAGLIOS: Sonnets.

3. SONGS OF LIFE AND DEATH.

4. THE POEMS OF FRANCIS VILLON. Now first done into English Verse.

5. LAUTREC: A Poem.

NEW POEMS.

MR. PAYNE AS A POET.

~~~~~~~~~~

" There is often an originality in Mr. Payne s poetry, a subtlety in his thought, a niceness in his language, and a melody in his versification, which at the present time we look for in vain in any but one or two of our leading poets."—*Saturday Review*.

" We must accord to the author of ' Lautrec ' a high and rare order of poetic genius."—*Examiner*.

" Mr. Payne belongs to that small body of cultivated men who will probably be the glory of Victorian literature, who have succeeded in wedding thought to new music. With Mr. Payne, as with Swinburne and Rossetti, the English language has become perfectly flexible. Further, he gives new beauty to the oldest subjects, and there cannot be a better test of a poet's power. There is, in short, nothing commonplace in Mr. Payne. He may not be popular with 'the blind multitude,' but he is sure to be so with all lovers of poetry, both to-day and to-morrow."—*The Westminster Review*.

" Of the great poetic power possessed by Mr. Payne there can be no question. The subtle beauty of his verse, its glowing passion and its rich diction, must be universally admitted."— *Literary World*.

" We should say that Mr. Payne is far more likely than Mr. Swinburne to be hailed, some few years hence, as the favourite poet of the now rising generation."—*Illustrated London News*.

" Mr. Payne's command of melodious language and imagina-tive power is undoubted ; and his place among modern poets is a high one."—*John Bull*.

MR. PAYNE'S WORKS.

———⸙⸙———

I.

Fcap. 8vo., cloth, 7s.

THE MASQUE OF SHADOWS AND OTHER POEMS.

" 'La Transfiguration des Ombres ' (si l'on peut ainsi traduire 'The Masque of Shadows') est un poëme dont la conception étrange rappelle les visions d'Edgar Poe, et dont l'harmonie imaginative est digne de Shelley. . . . . Telle est cette vision bizarre et grandiose. . . . . Ce qu'il y a de bonne ou de mauvaise philosophie en de pareilles imaginations, le lecteur l'appréciera. Mais nous pouvons lui dire et lui affirmer que l'auteur a fait là œuvre véritable de poésie. D'un noir cercueil il a évoqué un splendide bouquet de fleurs, légères comme les ailes de l'Espérance, fraîches et parfumées comme les lèvres du printemps. C'est vague, impalpable, diapré, immense et céleste ; tel l'arc en ciel rayonne après l'orage qui a dévasté. Encore une fois, il y a là de la poésie. On ne saurait demander plus à un poëte. Insensé ! si vous voulez ; mais certainement très-beau !"—*La Renaissance.*

" We gladly welcome Mr. Payne amongst that select number of poets that already comprises such names as Rossetti, Swinburne, and Morris."—*The Westminster Review.*

" Mr. Payne's 'Masque of Shadows' is a work of great refinement and beauty. . . . . Mr. Payne possesses great imaginative power and a wonderful command of language and rhythm. . . . . Striking as is the 'Rime of Redemption,' which has not unfitly been compared to the 'Ancient Mariner,' the next poem, 'The Building of the Dream,' is to our mind a yet more favourable specimen of Mr. Payne's powers. The opening sketch of the peaceful town in which the squire of Poitou dwelt is almost equal to Mr. Morris at his best, and this is the highest praise that can well be bestowed. Nor is the description of the seven days' journey towards the West less effective. . . . . When the seven days are passed, and Ebhardt wins his way at length to the land of dreams, we are presented with a series of pictures which almost cloy us with splendour and dazzle us with colour. Passage after passage might be quoted which for richness of language and brilliancy of imagination find few equals among the poetry of the day. The fault is that they are, taken together, a little too rich and splendid, but each taken by itself is exquisite in finish and full of grace and melody. . . . . Many a passage of beauty, with a tender and delicate fragrance breathing out of it. . . . . We recognise in Mr. Payne a poet of no mean order, one from whom we may expect great things in future, and who has already given us a work of great beauty and elegance."—*John Bull.*

"This is a book of genuine imagination; the qualities which characterize it are precisely those which distinguish poetry from less elevated forms of composition. Its most marked feature is an exuberance of fancy and invention, controlled by a chastened literary taste. . . . . 'The Rime of Redemption' is a wild legend in the form of a ballad, narrated with admirable point, and full of spirit and fire. 'The Building of the Dream' and 'Sir Floris' are successions of exquisite pictures. . . . . The volume abounds with proofs of culture and scholarship, no less than of poetical power."—*The Illustrated London News.*

"'The Masque of Shadows' has already won for Mr. Payne no mean place among the poets of the day."—*The Spectator.*

"A volume of uncommon merit. The story of Squire Ebhardt, in 'The Building of the Dream,' and of Sir Floris's winning his place among the guardians of the San Graal in the mystic city of Sarras, are very striking—and often very beautiful—reproductions of some of the best thought and best work of mediæval Christianity. Mr. Payne's lines abound with words of curious and semi-French archaism; but these are never dragged in; they suit the general effect, and clearly come from the overflow of a memory steeped in the romance literature whence they are drawn."—*The Saturday Review.*

"This curious and remarkable book is likely to win hearty appreciation from many who like to wander in the enchanted forests of poetry. In qualities of luxuriant grace and splendour of description Mr. Payne is eclipsed by few modern writers. In all metrical respects his verse is perfect. He has imagination, perception, and considerable lyrical power. There are in this book both promise and power."—*The Sunday Times.*

"Mr. Payne's 'Rime of Redemption' is vitalized by so true an imagination, it is so firm of texture and so rapid of movement, that it at once became a new possession to our ballad literature."—*Athenæum.*

3

II.

Fcap. 8vo., cloth, 3s. 6d.

INTAGLIOS: Sonnets.

"Mr. Payne is almost the best English sonnet writer that we have had since Mrs. Browning published her 'Sonnets from the Portuguese.' . . . . He writes like a poet, mastering the difficulties and satisfying the requirements of the sonnet with great skill. Here and there the antiqueness of his expression looks like affectation, but all flaws are atoned for by the exquisite thrills and touches of song he often utters."—*The Examiner.*

"Mr. Payne's chief characteristics are an exquisite tenderness and delicacy both of thought and of melody, a certain mystical tone and solemnity and a severely cultivated beauty of expression. . . . . We have not space to do justice to Mr. Payne's great merits, but to those who can read between the lines, the following delicious lyric will speak for itself." (*Sonnet* "Rococo" *quoted.*) "We cannot part with Mr. Payne without calling attention to the way in which he has reset many of our long-forgotten but beautiful expressions and archaisms. . . . . Mr. Payne's beautiful sonnet on Leconte de Lisle's Prose Translation of Homer may worthily be put side by side with Keats's sonnet on Chapman's Translation. . . . . Mr. Payne writes in the true spirit of that old poet—namesake of Homer's translator—who more than two centuries and a half ago thus spoke : 'A writer that dares venture, and is desirous to enrich his mother-tongue, decketh it boldly with that which he borroweth of others, (and) setteth forgotten words on foote againe' (LISLE, *Translation of Du Bartas* [1625], p. 71, foot-note.)"—*The Westminster Review.*

"There are few poems in the language in which the unseen has a more abiding presence, in which words are employed with more of suggestion, or in which the sympathy of inanimate nature with human suffering is more fully developed. In all sweet influences of nature Mr. Payne traces 'the still sad music of humanity,' and he displays remarkable power in conveying the influence which the soul in its moments of suffering or yearning is able to derive from the associations or caresses of nature. . . . . A certain misty fragrance of poetry, which is characteristic of all Mr. Payne's work, is prevalent in these sonnets. Added to this are a wealth, almost ostentatious, of language and great splendour of word-painting. . . . . Mr. Payne is an accomplished poet and a master of the form of composition he now essays. His work will be a delight to all who love beauty."—*Sunday Times.*

"We are grateful to Mr. Payne for rousing us from the somewhat drowsy state into which we had fallen as we perused page after page of poets gifted with that fatal fluency of language which is so convenient a cloak to the want of thought. If he is at times obscure, there is much in his sonnets that is as clear as it is beautiful. They show no signs of hasty work; on the contrary, they are polished as only a scholar loves to polish. . . . . Some of Mr. Payne's lines are wonderfully musical."—*Saturday Review*.

" In 'Intaglios' are noticeable the same features which elicited admiration and applause in 'The Masque of Shadows.' Elevation of thought and literary culture are combined with so delicate and airy a fancy that one is almost inclined to object to the hardness implied in the title, forgetting for the moment that the term is to be applied rather to the execution than to the material." —*Illustrated London News*.

"There is much that is noteworthy in these sonnets—subtle fancy, scholarly execution, and a quaintness of thought which, although occasionally more curious than beautiful, is not without a charm. Mr. Payne has more grace than strength, more of tenderness and refined feeling than of sustained power. He does not speak to the multitude, but the careful workmanship displayed in this little volume will excite the admiration of all students of poetry."—*Pall Mall Gazette*.

" The sonnet seems to suit the genius of Mr. Payne's poetry. Its narrow limits and the rigidity of its form do something to check the wild luxuriance of his fancy. But the intrinsic faults and beauties of such verse as he writes are of course not materially affected by any variation of form. A highly poetical style, made positively gorgeous by a word-painting which uses liberally the most brilliant colours, attracts the reader with great promise of beauty. Here is a sonnet that Mrs. Browning might have written. It is called 'Jacob and the Angel,' and is said to have been suggested by 'a design by J. T. Nettleship.'"—*The Spectator*.

"Mr. Simeon Solomon's sketch 'Sleepers, and One that Watches,' has been translated into verse of kindred strength and delicacy in three fine sonnets of high rank among the exquisite and clear-cut 'Intaglios' of Mr. John Payne."—ALGERNON C. SWINBURNE, *in " The Dark Blue*."

"Mr. Payne is already very favourably known to a certain cultivated section of the public as the author of 'The Masque of Shadows,' and some other shorter poems. Of the present little volume it would be difficult to speak in too high praise. Indeed we know of no sonnets which of late years have seen the light of day that can surpass 'Intaglios' either in beauty of conception or perfection of execution."— *Civilian*.

" To the few to whom a volume of sonnets is welcome, we can confidently recommend this little book. Mr. Payne has really something to say that could not be said in prose. His work conveys a genuine sense of mystery, and its changing lights and shadows are reflected from a truly artistic mind."—*The Guardian*.

III.

Crown 8vo., cloth, 5s.

SONGS OF LIFE AND DEATH.

" It is a perfect delight to meet with such a ballad as that of 'May Margaret' in the present volume. The art of ballad-writing has long been lost in England, and Mr. Payne may claim to be its restorer. Nor has Mr. Payne sacrificed any of those qualities, grace of style and delicacy of thought, which first of all won him so many admirers. He still writes with the same delight of the fields and the flowers and the spring, and still goes to the storehouse of our elder English poets for their old expressive words, which we have forgotten, and sets them with fresh beauty to modern thought."—*The Westminster Review.*

" That Mr. Payne is a poet has been proved by his earlier volumes, and is proved over again by this new collection of verse. His position is very creditable, and one from which he is able to sing very sweetly to all who have ears for musical and plaintive verse. . . . . 'A Birthday Song' is a good specimen of the very melodious strain in which Mr. Payne writes. . . . . Fancy, beyond all doubt, is strong in him, and he uses it in fantastic verse that is very charming. 'In Armida's Garden,' 'A Song of Roses,' and 'Into the Enchanted Land,' are very welcome specimens of the skill and grace with which he exhibits his vague philosophy. . . . . The best things in the volume are perhaps the ballads, and of these perhaps the best is 'The Ballad of May Margaret,' which we should like to quote entire. . . . . Surely if Mr. Payne had written nothing but this 'Ballad of May Margaret,' he would have made good his claim to be ranked among the poets."—*The Examiner.*

" There is much in Mr. Payne's present work that deserves high praise. . . . . There is often an originality in his poetry, a subtlety in his thoughts, a niceness in his language, and a melody in his versification, which at the present time we look for in vain in any but one or two of our leading poets. . . . . We can forgive Mr. Payne his occasional haziness, when he gives us such fine poems as 'The Ballad of Shameful Death,' 'Vocation Song,' 'Madrigal Triste,' and 'A Farewell.' "—*The Saturday Review.*

" 'Songs of Life and Death' form an important addition to our modern poetry. The ballads give evidence of great power, and 'The Westward Sailing' and 'May Margaret' will bear comparison with the ballads of any living poet."—*The School Board Chronicle.*

" In 'Songs of Life and Death' we feel the music-making force of an impassioned imagination, with its 'thoughts that voluntary move harmonious numbers.' This volume of genuine lyrics is a worthy successor to 'The Masque of Shadows' and

6

'Intaglios.' There is much power manifested here; and we should say Mr. Payne is far more likely than Mr. Swinburne to be hailed, some ten or twenty years hence, as the favourite poet of the now rising generation. 'The Westward Sailing,' 'The House of Sorrow,' and 'Sir Erwin's Questing,' are romantic narratives with a strong mystic fascination."—*The Illustrated London News.*

"Mr. Payne's 'Songs of Life and Death' are of a different order" [*from Longfellow's Three Books of Song, reviewed immediately before*]. "Clear, mellifluous, full of harmony and studied grace of expression, they deal with scarcely ordinary forms of experience; but though now and again touched with something of mediæval or mystical quaintness tending to affectation, have yet an absorbing sweetness and attraction. In such poems as 'A Song of Roses,' 'Into the Enchanted Land,' 'In Armida's Garden,' and 'A Song before the Gates of Death,' we have specimens of the mystical side of Mr. Payne's poetry, which has something slightly kindred to the better phases of Mr. Swinburne's genius. Mr. Payne exhibits not a little of Mr. Swinburne's wondrous craft of words, though exhibiting less recklessness, if we may speak so, and exercising more severity over the utterance of his moods than the other. Scarce anything can be finer than the two or three ballads which Mr. Payne has given us here, especially 'The Westward Sailing,' with which the volume opens—of itself almost enough to make a reputation."—*The Nonconformist.*

"Mr. Payne is one of the most melodious of our modern minstrels. The work before us, like its predecessors, contains passages of rare grace and beauty. . . . . Felicity of diction, refined taste and imaginative power, are a rare combination at all times, and eminently so in the present condition of poetry. All of these Mr. Payne possesses in no common degree. Thus a volume of poems from him is no ordinary treat. . . . . The author is perhaps most happy in treating such legends as 'The Westward Sailing,' 'The King's Sleep,' and 'Sir Erwin's Questing;' though 'False Spring,' 'Into the Enchanted Land,' 'A Bacchic of Spring,' and 'Cadences,' are very beautiful, and 'The Ballad of Shameful Death' is full of power."—*John Bull.*

"When Mr. Payne published some time since his first volume of poems, 'The Masque of Shadows,' etc., he was at once recognised as a poet of no mean capacity. Notwithstanding that he appeared before the public whilst the excitement caused by Mr. Rossetti's book was at its height, the artistic merits of his work were such as not merely to attract general attention, but to procure him a high rank among writers of imaginative poetry. The subsequent publication of 'Intaglios' more than confirmed his position, for while it exhibited to the fullest extent the same refinement of idea and musical grace of execution, it was comparatively free from a certain appearance of affectation which here and there characterised his first effort. . . . . There is a great variety of themes in the present volume. ' A Song before the Gates of Death ' exhibits a power of language hardly to have been suspected. . . . . ' False Spring ' embodies a charmingly poetical idea. . . . . In the ' Hymn to the Night ' a similar idea is treated in a different manner, but with equal beauty of imagery and fluency of versification. ' A Ballad of Shameful Death ' and and ' In the Night Watches ' are also remarkably good. ' A Birthday Song ' is a love poem absolutely perfect in its tenderness and grace. There is also ' A Song of Roses ' almost perfect in its way. . . . . Mr. Payne may be said to hold a position about midway between Mr. Rossetti and Mr. Swinburne. He has many qualities common to both masters, but he does not quite reach either the passionate intensity of the latter or the subtlety of the former. Thus his book is less involved and difficult than Mr. Rossetti's, whilst it is entirely free from the unconventionalities which exclude ' Poems and Ballads ' from the drawing-room table. In fact, ' Songs of Life and Death ' might be put into any schoolgirl's hands, not only without danger, but with the greatest advantage."—*The Civilian.*

"Mr. John Payne a publié, l'un après l'autre, trois livres délicieux : les ' Intaglios ' ou Camées, ' Le Masque de l'Ombre,' et les ' Chants de Vie et de Mort.' Nous prononçons avec joie ces titres en français, tels qu'ils seront un jour célèbres chez nous, une fois les poëmes traduits. . . . Il y a là, parmi ces strophes, même pour un regard étranger, des beautés particulières qui ne peuvent passer inaperçues. Cette poésie est un vibration musicale, prolongée de toute notre personne poétique. Avec une telle sensibilité, la part de la mélancolie est grande certainement, et parfois celle des extases fugitives et insaisissables. Une brume anglaise? Non, mais la vapeur diffuse du plus adorable jet d'eau lyrique, qui va se perdre dans l'air lumineux du ciel. On sait pendant ce temps-là qu'on songe irrésistiblement à la vie, aux adieux, à la mort, aux fleurs, à tout ce qui fait le fond de notre âme. Tout ceci est absolument *genuine*, comme on dit en Angleterre, où c'est le produit du pays : cependant nous nous y reconnaissons, nous aussi, à merveille. Cette impression familiale, disséminée dans les trois livres cités, se condense, à travers les pages du dernier, jusqu'à éclater, vers la fin, en un chant magnifique composé pour la France pendant l'hiver de 1870-1. Quelle courage il y avait alors à élever, seul, la voix pour nous, seul dans l'Angleterre et peut-être dans l'Europe ! Je transcris pieusement plusieurs fragments de cette ode *patriotique.*"—THEODORE DE BANVILLE dans le *National.*

"Ne vous est-il jamais arrivé de vous éveiller tout d'un coup au milieu d'un calme et délicieux clair de lune, après avoir été traîné à travers de ténébreuses angoisses par un méphistophélique cauchemar? Le sommeil pesait sur vous comme les murailles lourdes d'un noir cachot : vous aviez la sueur froide au front : un bourreau masqué vous donnait la torture. Vous vous êtes débattu, vous avez voulu fuir, et soudain, comme à un coup de

baguette magique, voilà le bourreau disparu, voilà les murailles
tombées. L'angoisse se dissipe, les ténèbres s'éclairent molle-
ment. Vous revenez peu à peu à la sérénité, et pour chasser
jusqu'au souvenir du démon qui vous tourmentait, vous ouvrez
votre fenêtre à l'air frais de la nuit. Là-bas, alors, perdu dans
les lilas obscurs, le rossignol vous chante une mélodieuse idylle,
et la musique de cette âme d'oiseau se fond autour de vous et en
vous avec le parfum des fleurs pudiques et le bleuâtre rayonne-
ment de l'nfiini céleste. Nous avons éprouvé une impression
semblable en échappant momentanément aux mélancolies de la
politique et à l'amertume des affaires sérieuses, pour nous plonger
dans le clair de lune poétique de John Payne, l'un des derniers
venus parmi les poëtes contemporains d'Angleterre. Adieu le
hideux cauchemar de la réalité humaine ! La Muse vêtue de
blanc et couronnée d'étoiles nous ouvre à deux battants la porte
d'or du palais enchanté de l'Idéal, et sur cette porte se lit cette
inscription : 'Vous qui entrez ici, quittez toute désespérance !' Si
les 'Intaglios' respirent une admiration sincère et un grande
expérience de l'art italien, les 'Chants de la Vie et de la Mort'
portent en eux un non moins profond amour et une science non
moins profonde de la poésie française, surtout des lyriques du
seizième et du dix-neuvième siècle. Le tempérament du poëte
n'est guères français, pourtant. S'il est épris de toute les déli-
catesses, de toutes les langueurs, de toutes les préciosités de la
forme, c'est pour en vêtir des sentiments mélancoliques, des idées
mystiques. C'est l'imagination septentionale éprise de l'art
latin. Il semble, en certains poëmes, qu'on entende gémir l'âme
de la Neige ou de la Brume, jalouse des citronniers en fleurs :
puis l'harmonie de certaines strophes évoque l'image de la Mort,
assise, au clair de la lune sur la pierre d'un tombeau, et qui rêve,
en effeuillant des roses rouges et blanches, aux chaudes amours
de Vénus la blonde, de l'immortelle enchanteresse Vénus. . . . .
'Les Chants de la Vie et de la Mort' commencent par une
belle ballade norvégienne, 'A la voile pour l'occident !'. . . .
A côté des ces fantastiques légendes s'épanouissent de pâles
élégies, des chansons d'une inspiration personnelle, des stances
d'un mélancolie caressante ou d'un harmonieux désespoir.
Tendres et délicates *fleurs de lune*, comme dit le poëte. . . . .
Puis il entonne un 'Chant devant les Portes de la Mort,' sorte
de défi à la souffrance et à l'inconnu, qui se résume en cette fière
parole : *Sed satis est jam posse mori* . . . . Il chante aussi 'La
Chanson des Roses,' avec une très-précieuse mélancolie, et
trouve des phrases si vaguement et si profondément mélodieuses,
qu'il nous semble voir et entendre la forme et la musique d'un
parfum. . . . . L'impuissance du désir, d'autant plus cruelle et
plus chère au cœur que la cœur qui désire est plus supérieur à
l'humanité, est admirablement exprimée dans la belle pièce dédiée
à Stéphane Mallarmé, 'l'Ame fantôme.' . . . . Nous avons pris
un plaisir particulier aux visions de John Payne. Il nous a
ouvert son âme de poëte, et nous y avons pénétré comme en un
pays nouveau, où chantent des mélodies inconnues, où s'épan-

9

ouissent des floraisons surnaturelles. . . . . Vos yeux, sont-ils
blessés par la clarté crue du soleil et les aspérités des choses ?
Allez vers ce poëte : il vous taillera en plein ciel des lunettes
suprêmement bleues, sous lesquelles tout se calmera, tout s'attend-
rira pour vous. . . . . Il a, pour employer son langage, pressé
son cœur comme une grappe mûre, et il en est coulé de la poésie,
de la vraie poésie."—*La Renaissance.*

IV.

*Small quarto, printed on hand-made paper and bound in vellum,
gilt, frontispiece and facsimiles.*

THE POEMS OF MASTER FRANCIS VILLON
OF PARIS.

Now first done into English verse in the original forms.
(Printed for private circulation only.—Exhausted.)

" Quel honneur vous faites à la France et quel présent admirable vous offrez à l'Angleterre ! Grâce à vous, elle a un poëte
et un bien grand poëte de plus : et tout en lui gardant essentielle-
ment son âme gauloise, vous avez bien fait de Villon un des
vôtres et pour toujours. Plût à Dieu que nous eussions chez
nous des artistes capables de réaliser de telles merveilles et de
franciser magistralement vos grands compatriotes ! . . . . J'ad-
mire, au-delà de tout, à quel point vous avez su garder le mouve-
ment, le rhythme, la sonorité, l'aspect visible, tout l'être de
notre Villon. Non, ceci n'est pas une traduction, c'est un
Villon anglais qui est né ; à présent il est à vous comme à nous."
—THEODORE DE BANVILLE.

V.

Fcap. 8vo. 3s. 6d.

LAUTREC: A POEM.

"Mr. Payne belongs to that small body of cultivated men
who will probably be the glory of Victorian literature, who have
succeeded in wedding thought to new music. His fine poem of
' Lautrec' thoroughly removes the objections that his critics
have, not perhaps without reason, made to his former works, *i.e.*
that he failed to get a firm grip of his subject, and mostly dwelt
in a region of twilight. . . . . Everywhere is the poem characterised by complete mastery of the rhythm and the rhyme : the
English language has become with Mr. Payne, as with Swinburne and Rossetti, perfectly flexible. Further, he gives new
beauty to the oldest subjects, and there cannot be a better test
of a poet's power. . . . . There is, in short, nothing common-

place in Mr. Payne. He may not be 'popular with the 'blind multitude,' but he is sure to be so with all lovers of poetry both to-day and to-morrow."—*The Westminster Review.*

"The treatment of the legend is both powerful and poetical."—*Athenæum.*

"There are passages in this poem which nothing in modern poetry, French or English, can surpass. Nothing can be more repulsive than portions of the treatment, yet all remains within the limits of art. We pay Mr. Payne a compliment, the full value of which he will admit, in likening his work to that of the painter, Henri Regnault. . . . . That highest of poetic gifts, imagination, is present. It will be considered by many an 'imagination unblessed,' but its presence will not be disputed. It is easy to furnish passages of great power and of beauty also. Still, the book is one to be read in its integrity. It is very short, and the task to the lover of poetry will be both light and pleasurable."—*Sunday Times.*

"Mr. Payne's command of melodious language and imaginative power are undoubted, and his place among modern poets is a high one."—*John Bull.*

"We must accord to the author of 'Lautrec' a high and rare order of poetic genius."—*Examiner.*

"Of the great poetic power possessed by Mr. Payne there can be no question. The subtle beauty of his verse, its glowing passion and its rich diction are universally admitted."—*Literary World.*

"How is it that a theme which would be simply weird and horrible, if not even directly repulsive, in prose, may be not only tolerable, but 'beautiful exceedingly,' in poetry, under the master's hand? Many reasons might be given, but there is this cogent one, namely, that whatever may be ghastly and repulsive in the subject is softened in the moonlight of the poet's fancy, and so related, by suggestions of rhythm and of sweet and subtle sounds, to the higher order of feeling, that all impression of the distorted and *eerie* in itself is swallowed up in the very unity of impression that poetry must seek after. This is well illustrated in Mr. Payne's new poem of 'Lautrec,' in which the author shows all his old art in connecting fresh pictures of natural aspects of things with the exhibition of morbid phantasy. He has the art of the poet, and the horrible is artistically kept in subordination to the human feeling, the protest of the heart against the doom being the burden of the poem. We need not add that the style is simple and effective, sometimes gracefully quaint."—*Nonconformist.*

www.ingramcontent.com/pod-product-compliance
Lightning Source LLC
Chambersburg PA
CBHW060532030726
47498CB00004B/1162